S.CREAM SHOP

Three Strikes and You're a Monster!

By Tracey West

This book is dedicated to the memory of my grandmother, Ruth, a Mets fan who introduced me to the joys of baseball—T.W.

For my sister Kathi, who encouraged me years ago that children's book illustration was where my destiny was to be found—B.D.

Copyright © 2004 by Tracey West. Illustrations copyright © 2004 by Brian W. Dow. All rights reserved. Published by Grosset & Dunlap, a division of Penguin Young Readers Group, 345 Hudson Street, New York, New York 10014. GROSSET & DUNLAP is a trademark of Penguin Group (USA) Inc. Printed in the U.S.A.

Library of Congress Cataloging-in-Publication Data is available.

ISBN 0-448-43359-1   A B C D E F G H I J

S.CREAM SHOP

Three Strikes and You're a Monster!

By Tracey West

Illustrated by Brian W. Dow

MAY   2006

Grosset & Dunlap • New York

"Look alive out there, boys!" Coach Johnson yelled. "This is baseball practice, not nap time!"

The players in the outfield responded to the coach by adjusting their hats, clapping their hands, or shifting from one foot to another. They all had their eyes on home plate, where a batter stood, his bat held firmly in his hands.

The pitcher threw a fastball at the batter. It came in a little low, but the batter swung.

Crack! The ball sailed toward right field. The fielder ran to catch it, but he wasn't fast enough. The ball bounced on the grass a good ten feet in front of him. The infielder scrambled toward the ball, scooped it up, and hurled the ball to second base—seconds too late.

"Safe!" yelled the coach. He turned to the right fielder. "You call that looking alive?"

On the edge of the field, a boy watched the practice through the fence.

"I could have caught that," Matt Carter muttered. He kicked a rock with his sneaker and watched it go clattering down the sidewalk.

It just wasn't fair, Matt thought to himself. All summer, he had dreamed of playing for the Ravens, the August Bleaker Elementary School baseball team. He pictured himself standing in the field, wearing the Ravens' black uniform. The batter would hit the ball to the outfield, and he'd jump up so high, his arm raised above his head, and then, *wham*! He'd catch the ball neatly in his glove as the crowd clapped and cheered. Matt could catch just about anything, no matter how high or how fast it was hurtling toward him.

"We'll be watching you play in the big leagues one day," his dad always said, whenever they played catch in the yard. "My son, Gabriel Matthew Carter, a major-league star."

Matt loved to hear him say that—even though he hated when his dad called him by his full name. Matt had always liked to be called by his middle name much better. It sounded more like a baseball name to him.

With his sights on the big leagues, Matt joined the Pee Wee leagues when he was just four years old. He played on the junior elementary team every season, and he caught just about every ball that came his way.

There was only one problem.

Matt couldn't hit.

He tried. He placed his hands on the bat exactly where the coach told him to. He never took his eye off the ball. He would watch it coming, a white blur spiraling through the air, and then he'd swing . . . and miss. Just about every time. Or if he did hit the ball, it went careening in some crazy direction, usually hitting the umpire or somebody in the stands.

Matt's lousy hitting hadn't mattered so much on the junior league. They let anybody play. But Matt was in sixth grade now, and to get on the Ravens, you had to try out. They were a good team, and had made it to the state finals for the last three years. Matt had tried out last week, but didn't make the team.

"The last thing they need is a strikeout king like me," Matt said, sighing. He turned away from the practice and began to walk home.

Matt decided to take the long way. He had nothing better to do. He had never learned an instrument, so he couldn't go to band practice, and all of the paperboy jobs had been taken already.

"Just keep practicing," his dad had said. "You'll get on the team next year."

But Matt didn't see the point. No matter how hard he tried, he couldn't make contact with the ball. His father said he just needed more confidence. But how was he supposed to get confidence when he couldn't play with the Ravens?

Matt headed downtown. There wasn't much to do anywhere in Bleaktown, and downtown wasn't much better. But the stationery store on Main Street sold comic books and baseball cards, and he might find his friend Jason there. Matt dug into his jeans pocket and pulled out a few crumpled bills. Enough for a couple of comics—he didn't really feel like buying baseball cards today.

He turned down a side street and glanced at the stores there. He passed a window display of lampshades. Another window held metal canes and walkers and other medical devices.

"Boring Bleaktown," Matt muttered.

The next store window held a statue of a crocodile, a battered wizard's hat, an old toy fire truck, a row of round, glass globes, and two baseball bats, arranged like an X, leaning up against an ancient-looking shield.

Matt stopped. What kind of store was this? It didn't seem like it belonged in Bleaktown. He glanced at the sign in the window that read, "Sebastian Cream's Junk Shop."

That's funny, Matt thought. *I never noticed this place before.*

Everything in the store's window looked interesting. But Matt found himself drawn to the baseball bats.

One was made of wood and looked very old, but the wood was smooth and polished so it shone. The other was made of metal, but it didn't look like anything Matt had ever seen before. Its sleek shape wasn't quite that of a baseball bat, and the silver color of the metal seemed to be rippling, almost like it was moving.

Why are you looking at the bats, anyway? a little voice inside him asked. *You know you can't hit.*

Maybe I just haven't had the right bat, Matt answered himself. *Every great player has a lucky bat, right? Maybe I just haven't found mine yet.*

Matt stepped back from the window. He probably couldn't afford either bat.

Still, it couldn't hurt to ask, could it?

Matt walked up the step and opened the shop door. A bell chimed as he stepped inside.

A little man walked up to him. Everything about him was round, from the shape of his belly to the round rims of his glasses to the ring of white hair circling his bald head.

"I assume you're here about the baseball bats," the man said.

"How did you know?" Matt asked, startled.

The man smiled. "It's my job to know what my customers want. Let me fetch the bats for you."

Mr. Cream climbed into the window display and returned with a bat in each hand. He gave them both to Matt.

"They are each quite special," he said. "I

imagine you'll have a difficult time choosing."

"I, uh, I don't know if I can get one," Matt said. "I probably can't afford one."

Mr. Cream smiled. "Well, it's your lucky day," he said. "I am having a sale on sports equipment today." He named a price, and Matt knew he had enough money in his pocket for one bat—but only one.

"I guess I can afford one after all," Matt said excitedly. "Can I try them out?"

The little man nodded. "Of course," he said. "Why don't you come over here and take some practice swings before you decide." His green eyes twinkled behind his glasses. "But choose carefully."

Matt picked up the wooden bat first. He found a space between two shelves in the crowded store and took a slow-motion swing. The wood felt good in his hands, like it had been made just for him.

"Very traditional," Mr. Cream said. "Old-school, as you young people might call it."

Matt tried the metal bat next. It didn't feel quite as comfortable as the first one, but it made his hands kind of . . . tingle. And there was something about the sleek design that made it look like the bat could hit anything, and send it soaring into the stands.

"Ah, now that is the latest in baseball bat technology," Mr. Cream said. "You'd certainly get attention with that bat."

Matt held a bat in each hand and looked at them. He couldn't decide.

"So, young man," Mr. Cream said. "Which will it be?"

If Matt chooses the sleek metal bat, go to page 62.

If Matt chooses the old wooden bat, go to page 18.

Continued from page 40

"Let's start with the first cave," Matt suggested.

Jason nodded and aimed his flashlight at the first cave opening. But the tiny light didn't reveal anything except for darkness. Matt suddenly felt nervous about going inside.

Jason must have felt the same way.

"You go first," he told Matt.

Matt took a deep breath. It was his baseball bat, after all. The only way to find out why the bat had made him grow fur and play baseball better was to step inside that cave.

Matt stepped inside—and immediately felt something squishy under his foot.

"Gross!" he cried, jumping back.

Jason shone his flashlight on the ground. A green, slimy substance covered the floor of the cave. He moved his flashlight up and saw that the slime dripped down from the walls.

"Great," Matt groaned. "It's like a snot party in here."

Matt stepped farther inside, with Jason following behind him. Thanks to the dim light of Jason's penlight, they could see that they were in a kind of tunnel—a tunnel leading down into the earth.

"Do you really want to go down there?" Jason

asked. "Maybe we should try one of the other caves."

"We came this far," Matt argued. "We should at least see what's here."

Jason thought. "Okay. How about if we walk and I count to a hundred? If we don't see anything by the time I'm finished, we'll turn back."

Matt nodded. "All right."

Matt led the way. Behind him, he heard Jason counting softly under his breath.

They walked on and on, with no sign of anything but slime. Jason was nearing the end of his count.

"Ninety-six. Ninety-seven. Ninety-eight. Ninety-nine." Jason paused. Matt lifted his foot to take the last step. "One hundred!"

And then, suddenly, they were both falling, plummeting down a slippery slide! The green ooze splashed in Matt's face as he fell. It tasted salty and bitter on his tongue.

Finally, he landed with a thud on a cold, stone floor. Jason slammed into his back. Matt slowly stood up.

When he looked up, he screamed in horror. He found himself face to face with a hideous creature! It towered over them. Matted brown fur covered its body. Two huge, green eyes glowed from its face. Two horns curved from the top of its head, brushing the top of the cave.

But the worst thing of all was its mouth: a huge, snarling maw filled with dozens of sharp fangs!

"What's the matter?" the creature asked. "Haven't you ever seen a monster before?"

If Matt and Jason run, go to page 25.

If Matt and Jason ask the monster about the baseball bat, go to page 41.

Continued from page 113

The men looked so official that Matt almost gave him the bat.

But then he thought to himself, *Why should I give it over? It's my lucky bat.* He quickly turned around and ran back into the stadium.

Behind him, he heard the men take after him on foot. From the corner of his eye, Matt saw two security guards come out and stop the two men. Matt watched from a safe distance as the men argued with the guards, who refused to let them in. The men reluctantly headed back to their car.

Matt waited for his dad outside Mr. Hamilton's office. Matt's dad came out looking excited.

"Harry wants you to play in an exhibition game next week," he said. "Isn't that great?"

"Sure, Dad," Matt said, but he kept thinking about the mysterious men. He suddenly remembered Jason's cousin Arnold. He reached into the front pocket of his jeans, which he hadn't washed since that day on the practice field. The crumpled note was still there. As Matt and his dad walked to the car, Matt unfolded the note and read it again.

Maybe Jason's cousin would be able to tell him about the guys in blue. It was worth a try, anyway. As soon as he got home, Matt hopped on his bike and headed to the Peanut Brittle Factory.

The place looked like an old-fashioned candy shop. Matt walked in and found Jason's cousin inside. Arnold stood behind the counter. His black beret and serious face looked strange among the bins of brightly colored candy.

"You're late," Arnold said, frowning. "Did you bring the bat?"

Matt nodded.

Arnold walked to the front door, locked it, and turned the "OPEN" sign hanging in the window to read "CLOSED." Then he beckoned for Matt to follow him.

Arnold went to a wall stacked with bins of peanut brittle. He carefully pushed on one of the bins, and the wall swung aside. Arnold walked through the opening, and Matt followed.

Behind the wall was what looked like some kind of control center filled with computers, screens, and other strange-looking machines. A black-haired woman with glasses and a tall man with red hair were busily typing on keyboards.

"This is Matt," Arnold said simply. "He has the bat."

Before the two could reply, a loud crash came from the candy store. Arnold turned to Matt.

"Did anyone follow you here?"

Matt thought of the men in the black car he

saw earlier and cringed. "Maybe," he admitted.

"We should give them the bat," said the red-haired guy. "It's what they want."

"No way!" Matt exclaimed. "It's my bat. I say we run for it!"

If Matt lets Arnold and his friends have the bat, go to page 45.

If Matt convinces the others to run for it, go to page 30.

Matt took a deep breath. "I'll take this one," he said, holding out the old bat made of wood. He liked how comfortable it felt.

Sebastian Cream nodded and took the metal bat from Matt.

"The wooden bat suits you," Mr. Cream said. "I think you made the right choice."

Matt paid for the bat, thanked Mr. Cream, and headed right to Jason's house. He knew his best friend would be just as excited about the bat as he was.

Jason's family had one of the nicer houses in Bleaktown. The white, two-story house sat on a green lawn wide enough and long enough to hold a baseball diamond. Mr. Hamilton, Jason's father, sat at a table on the front porch, looking over some papers. He waved his hand at Matt.

"Jason's upstairs," Mr. Hamilton said. Matt nodded and ran up to Jason's room.

He found his friend sitting at his desk. Piles of baseball cards were stacked neatly in front of him.

"Hey," he said when Matt entered. "I'm re-organizing my cards. I'm almost done."

"I thought you had them organized already,"

Matt said, plopping down on a red beanbag chair on the floor.

"They were organized by team," Jason said. "But now I'm organizing them by position. I've got all the pitchers in that pile, see? I just can't decide whether to order them by their winning percentage or ERA."

Matt shook his head. Jason didn't play baseball—but he was the biggest baseball fan Matt knew. He loved keeping track of players' statistics, and he knew every rule of the game inside out. Matt guessed it was probably because Jason's dad owned the Hornets, a minor-league team. Jason had been raised on baseball.

Jason put down the pile of cards he was sorting through and looked at Matt. He raised an eyebrow when he saw the bat.

"Hey, what's that?" he asked, getting off his chair. He took the bat from Matt and examined it.

"I found it in this crazy shop downtown," Matt said. "Pretty cool, huh?"

"It looks pretty old," Jason said thoughtfully. "It's probably made of white ash wood. That's very durable."

He turned to Matt. "Do you want to try it out?"

Matt suddenly felt nervous. He'd probably

strike out with this bat—just like he always did.

"Well, your dad's outside . . ." Matt said. He didn't want to embarrass himself in front of Mr. Hamilton.

"Don't worry. My dad already knows you can't hit," Jason said.

"Hey!" Matt said, punching Jason lightly on the arm. The boys laughed and headed outside.

Soon, Matt was facing Jason out on the front lawn. Jason didn't like to play, but he was a decent pitcher.

Matt took a deep breath. He held up the bat, keeping his hands together and low on the bat, like his dad had always taught him. He bent his legs slightly. Then he made sure he kept both eyes on Jason.

Jason threw the ball. Matt watched as the white blur sped toward him. He swung the bat, and, *crack*! The ball rolled across the ground and zipped right between Jason's legs. He had to run to catch it.

"Not bad!" he said, returning to the spot on the lawn he used as a pitcher's mound. "You hit it!"

Matt couldn't believe it. He had hit the ball. A grounder. Not a bad one, either.

It had to be a fluke.

"Pitch me another one," Matt said.

Jason sent another pitch sailing his way. Matt

hit it again. This time, it popped up into what would have been the infield.

"Keep 'em coming!" Matt yelled to his friend. He felt full of energy. Like he could hit anything. Maybe this was the confidence his dad had been talking about.

Jason pitched a few more to Matt, and Matt hit almost all of them. He was having so much fun, he didn't notice Mr. Hamilton walk up to them.

"You're looking good, Matt," he said. "Coach Johnson is lucky to have you on the Ravens."

"Actually, I didn't make the team," Matt said, looking down at his sneakers.

"Nonsense!" Mr. Hamilton said. "Brad Johnson is an old friend of mine. I'll give him a call tonight. I don't know what he could have been thinking."

Matt didn't even bother to explain. What would he say? *When I tried out, I couldn't hit a thing. But then I bought a lucky bat at a weird store, and now I can hit?* It sounded crazy.

Mr. Hamilton kept his word. The next day in gym class, Coach Johnson pulled Matt aside and told him to show up for baseball practice later that day.

Matt couldn't believe his luck. During lunch, he polished his bat until it shone.

"Whatever you did yesterday, please do it again," Matt whispered to the bat.

He and Jason were sitting together at their usual lunch table. Jason watched Matt and raised one eyebrow.

"Uh, I was just—" Matt said.

"Talking to your bat," Jason finished for him. "It's not unusual, actually. Many players talk to their bats. I wonder what the percentage of that is? I'll have to look into that."

When the final bell rang, Matt ran out to the practice field. His palms were sweating. This was his last chance to make the team. He couldn't mess up.

Coach Johnson nodded when he saw Matt.

"Let me toss a few balls to you while the rest of the guys are suiting up," he said. "I just hope Hamilton knows what he's talking about."

"Sure," Matt said.

Matt stood by home plate, lifted his bat, and watched Coach Johnson on the pitcher's mound. The beefy, blond-haired coach looked more like a football tackle than a baseball player. But he sailed a smooth pitch right over the plate.

Crack! Matt sent the ball flying into the outfield.

Coach Johnson looked impressed. "Not bad, Carter. Let's try again."

The coach pitched a few more balls, and Matt made contact with almost all of them. Finally, Coach Johnson walked up to the plate to talk to Matt.

"Hamilton was right," he said. "You must have just had an off day at tryouts, Carter. You're on the team."

That night, Matt felt happier than he had ever been. His mom and dad took Matt and his little sister, Kayla, out for pizza to celebrate. When he went to sleep that night, he tucked the bat under the covers next to him.

"You're not leaving my sight," Matt said as he drifted off to sleep.

As soon as the first rays of sun shone through the window, Matt jumped out of bed. Today was his first full day as a player for the Ravens. He didn't want to miss a minute of it. He tore off his pajamas and headed for the shower.

Then he stopped.

There was something covering his arms and legs. Was it dirt? Matt rubbed his left arm.

It wasn't dirt. It felt like . . . fur.

Matt looked in the mirror. His arms and legs were covered with some kind of brown fur! But where had it come from?

He slowly turned and looked back at the bed. Could the bat have something to do with it?

Maybe it was some kind of fungus or something!

"Oh, no!" Matt said to himself. "I *have* to play with the Ravens today!"

Matt knew he had to get to the bottom of this, and quick!

If Matt takes the bat back to the Scream Shop to ask Mr. Cream about it, go to page 77.

If Matt asks Jason to take another look at the bat, go to page 36.

Both boys screamed. Matt tried to climb back up the slippery tunnel. He could hear Jason behind him, trying to do the same thing.

Then Matt felt sharp claws dig into his left arm. He turned to look behind him. The monster gripped him in one of its hands, and Jason in another. Matt struggled to get out of the monster's powerful grasp, but it was no use.

"Not so fast," the monster said in a surprisingly smooth voice. "I'm sure you boys came here for something. Why don't you tell me what you're looking for?"

The monster released its grip, and Matt and Jason fell to the floor with a thud. The baseball bat slid out of Matt's backpack and clattered across the cold stone floor.

"Ah, yes," the monster said, smiling. It picked up the bat. "One of my earlier works. Quite amusing, really. It gives the user the ability to play baseball, but has the unfortunate side effect of turning him into a beast!"

The monster leaned back its head and laughed.

"A beast?" Matt asked. "So is that why I started getting all furry?"

Matt pushed up his shirt sleeve to reveal the fur. The monster nodded. "Yes, but it will fall off soon enough if you stop using the bat."

Matt's head was spinning. The monster seemed nice enough, even if it did look horrible. And finding out that his fur wasn't permanent gave him some relief.

"Uh, thanks," Matt said. "So I guess Jason and I should be going now. Is there another way out of here?"

The monster's green eyes flashed. Its mouth opened up into a wide grin—but it was a sinister smile, not a happy one.

"Oh, but you see, that is a problem," the monster said. "You have found my lair. It would be foolish of me to let you go. You'd only cause trouble for me. No, I'm sorry, but I'm afraid I'll have to keep you trapped down here."

Matt's heart skipped a beat. The monster sounded serious. He turned to Jason, expecting to see his friend as nervous as he was. But Jason looked thoughtful.

"Isn't that against the rules?" Jason asked.

The monster frowned. "What do you mean?"

"I read a book about monsters once," Jason explained. "You're a Vashlock, aren't you?"

The monster raised a hairy eyebrow. "That's right," it said.

"Vashlocks have the power to grant wishes to humans," Jason said. "But they have to follow rules. Strict rules."

"Wretched public library systems," the monster muttered, scowling. It sighed. "Yes, you are right."

Jason's voice got more confident now. "And rule number three-fifty-seven states that a Vashlock has to give humans a chance to escape before it captures them by offering them a challenge. If the humans win the challenge, they are allowed to go free."

Silently, Matt thanked Jason for his photographic memory. He started to believe that his friend could really get them out of this.

The monster scratched its chin with one of its right hands. "I've always hated that rule," it sighed. "But a rule is a rule. Let's see. What sort of challenge shall I give you?"

"How about we each pick a challenge, and the best of three wins?" Jason suggested.

The monster's eyes shone. "I like the sound of that," it said. "We'll do my event first—arm wrestling!" The Vashlock blinked, and a wooden table appeared. It placed its enormous arms on the table.

"Are you ready?" it asked Matt and Jason.

Matt and Jason exchanged looks. Matt stood

on one side of the monster, and Jason stood on the other. The monster grabbed Matt's arm with one of its powerful arms, and grabbed Jason's with another.

"Go!" the Vashlock called gleefully.

Wham! The monster slammed their arms down on the table in a split second. They didn't even have a chance.

"That was fun," the monster said. "What will it be next? Weight lifting?"

"It's my turn to choose," Jason said. "And I choose a trivia challenge: batting statistics of Hornets players."

The monster frowned. "The Hornets? Who cares about some minor-league team?"

"That's my dad's team," Jason said defensively. "And I get to choose the next challenge. So let's go at it."

The second contest didn't last long. Jason knew every statistic about every Hornets player who had ever lived. Even the monster's magical powers couldn't help him win the contest.

So the monster had won one contest. Jason had won the other. Now it was up to Matt to be the tiebreaker.

It was all up to Matt now. The Vashlock turned to him. Its hideous face looked very unhappy.

"Your turn," it said. "But I suspect you are not

as clever as your friend here. Tell me, what is your challenge?"

Matt thought about it. The only thing he was good at was catching fly balls. Maybe he could do something with that.

Then another idea popped into Matt's mind. A trick. He could try to trick the monster. But was it too risky?

If Matt tries to trick the monster, go to page 51.

If Matt challenges the monster to a catching contest, go to page 79.

"We can't run from the S.R.A.," said the black-haired woman. "They're too powerful."

Arnold looked thoughtful. "You're right, Onyx," he said. His eyes traveled to the bat sticking out of Matt's backpack. "We can't run. But maybe there's another way."

The crashing noises from the candy store got louder. It was only a matter of time before the men in blue came crashing into the secret room.

"S.R.A.? What are you talking about? What's going on?" Matt felt like he was in some kind of crazy movie.

"S.R.A. stands for Secret Recovery Agency, a top-secret branch of the government," Arnold said quickly. "They're here for the bat. That bat is an amazing piece of technology."

Matt shook his head. "This is too weird. Let's get out of here!"

"The bat can save us, Matt," Arnold said, holding out his hand. "You've got to trust me."

For a second, Matt was reminded of Jason when he looked into Arnold's serious brown eyes. He knew he could believe Arnold.

"Okay," Matt said, handing over the bat.

Arnold held out the bat. "I need everyone to

hold onto the bat," he said. "Use both hands."

"Do you really think it will work?" Howdy asked nervously.

"We've got to try," Arnold said.

Matt and the others wrapped their hands around the bat.

Then everything happened at once.

With a sickening, splintering sound, the men in blue burst through the wall into the secret room. Arnold pressed something on the bat's handle. Matt couldn't see what it was. And then a brilliant red light filled the room, blinding them.

Then Matt blinked. They were out in the sunshine. But they weren't in the candy shop. Or even near it.

They were standing on the roof of the Bleaktown Library!

Matt found that he was gripping the bat so tightly, his knuckles were white. He slowly let go.

"What just happened?" he asked Arnold.

"This bat is really a matter transporter, created by one of the world's most brilliant scientists, Leon Shingle," Arnold explained. "Shingle disguised it as a baseball bat so the government wouldn't find out about it. He didn't want them to use it for things like spying or war activity. But they got a hold of it, anyway."

"Cool," Matt said. Then he realized something.

"So, I guess I can't use it as a bat anymore?"

Arnold shook his head. "We're taking it back to Dr. Shingle. You're a hero, Matt. We couldn't have done it without you."

Hero. Matt liked the sound of that. It was almost better than major-league baseball player.

Matt smiled. "No problem!"

THE END

Continued from page 131

"Forget it, Jason," Matt said. "I'm not giving up now."

"But, Matt," Jason said. "It's all right here—"

"I said no, Jason," Matt replied.

"But all we have to do is—"

"I SAID NO!"

The words came out of Matt like a thundering roar. He stopped himself.

Jason looked terrified. He bundled his books in his arms and backed out of the door.

"Jason, I'm sorry," Matt said. "I don't know what happened. Maybe we can—"

"Forget it, Matt," Jason whispered. "There's no way to help you now."

Jason ran down the stairs and slammed the door behind him.

Matt looked in his bedroom mirror. Was he really turning into a beast, like the one in Jason's book?

"It's not real," Matt told his reflection. "I'll be just fine."

The next game was a few days later. The Ravens were playing the Pirates, another team from Smithville. Coach Johnson had Matt batting fourth again.

The stands were crowded with people from Bleaktown and Smithville who had heard about the new hotshot player on the Ravens. When Matt came out to bat the first time, the crowd erupted in a cheer. Matt didn't let them down. His very first hit was a home run.

Matt played the game of a lifetime. He hit three home runs. He hit the last one in the ninth inning, winning the game for the Ravens with a score of 16-3.

Matt rounded the bases, waving to the cheering crowd. He felt great, like he was floating on air.

He was the best baseball player in the world. He would go on to a career in the pros, for sure. Years from now, people would be paying millions just to own one of his home-run balls.

Just as Matt stepped onto home plate, he saw something up in the stands, in the very last row.

It was the monster. It held a pom-pom in each one of its clawed hands, and it was cheering Matt's name.

Matt's blood ran cold. He froze on home plate.

Something was happening.

His skin felt like it was burning with fever. It itched like crazy. Matt scratched his arms, and saw that his fingernails had turned into long, black claws.

"NOOOOOOOO!" Matt roared.

The crowd went silent. Matt tore at his baseball shirt, ripping it from his chest. Thick, brown fur pushed its way through Matt's skin, covering every inch of his body. He could feel it on his face, under his arms, between his fingers.

The people in the stands began to scream and run. Confused, Matt ran toward them.

Then he caught his reflection in the metal watercooler.

The face of a hideous beast stared back at him!

THE END

Matt didn't know what to do. If he told his mom and dad, they'd probably take him to the doctor, and he hated going there.

Then he remembered. Jason seemed to know a lot about the bat. If the bat was causing the fur or whatever it was, Jason might know why.

Matt quickly dressed, putting on jeans and a long-sleeved shirt to cover the fur. He carefully put the bat in a plastic trash bag and wrapped the bag around it. Then he ran to Jason's house.

He pounded on the door. Jason answered, still wearing his pajamas. He held a bowl of cereal in one hand.

"Mom and Dad are still asleep," Jason said. "What are you doing here so early?"

Matt pulled Jason out onto the front porch. Then he pulled up his sleeve.

"I have this fur or something all over me," Matt said. "I think I got it from the bat."

Jason leaned over and examined Matt's arm. "Looks like fur to me," he said. "You really think the bat did that?"

"I don't know," Matt said. "Maybe I'm allergic to that wood or something."

Matt handed the plastic-wrapped bat to Jason.

Jason put his cereal bowl down on the porch table and picked it up. "I never heard of anyone being allergic to a baseball bat," he said. "If it was possible, you think it would have happened to at least one major-league player."

Jason took the bat out of the plastic bag. He held it up to his nose and smelled it. He looked closely at every inch of the wood.

"Looks normal to me," he said. He went to hand the bat back to Matt.

Then he stopped.

"That's weird," he said. "The handle feels loose."

Jason gripped the bat and twisted the handle. Normally, the handle and bat were carved from the same piece of wood, but this handle screwed right off with a few turns.

"It's hollow," Jason said. "At least, for a few inches. And there's something in here."

Jason pulled out a yellowed piece of paper. He gingerly opened it. Matt leaned over his shoulder. Someone had drawn a map using thick, black ink. It looked really old-fashioned. But Matt recognized the location.

"It's a map of a place called the Harding Hills," Matt said.

"I know where that is!" Jason exclaimed. "My family and I go hiking there sometimes."

Matt scratched the fur on his arms. It was starting to itch.

"We've got to check out the Harding Hills," he said. "If this bat is the reason why I'm furry, I want to find out."

"Why not?" Jason said. "I'm pretty curious myself. Maybe this leads to some kind of baseball treasure or something."

"Can we go today?" Matt asked. "I can't stand this fur much longer."

Jason agreed, and an hour later, the boys hopped on their bikes and headed out to the Harding Hills. The morning sun grew hotter as they rode. Matt wished he hadn't had to wear a long-sleeved shirt. But he'd rather be hot than let anybody see his fur.

Finally, after about an hour, Jason stopped. The paved road had ended. In front of them lay a dirt road surrounded by trees.

"We're almost there," Jason said. "The map says that we have to take this trail."

Before he entered the trail, Matt gazed up at the hills. The three hills rose into the sky like the humps on a sea serpent's back. Each hill was covered with trees. Some of the trees had lost their leaves already, but many still blazed in shades of red, orange, and yellow. Compared to Bleaktown, the Harding Hills looked pretty cheerful. He wondered what the map could possibly lead to.

Matt pedaled ahead, keeping behind Jason. He bounced in his seat as his bike ran over rocks in the dirt path.

And then the path ended, just like that. They had reached the base of one of the hills.

"What now?" Matt asked.

Jason shrugged. "I don't know," he said. "The map doesn't say."

Matt scanned the scene in front of them. There were lots of trees and green plants. It didn't look like a place that would have anything to do with a mysterious baseball bat.

Then he noticed something odd.

"Over there," Matt said, pointing. "It looks like a cave."

They couldn't take their bikes any farther, so Matt and Jason leaned them up against two trees. They pushed some shrubs aside and headed to the cave entrance.

Matt had never seen a real cave before. It was pitch-black inside, and for a second Matt wondered if coming out to the Harding Hills had been a good idea. Caves were usually filled with spiders or bears or other dangerous things, weren't they?

"What do you think is in there?" Matt asked.

"There's one way to find out," Jason said. He took a pocket flashlight off his belt loop and shone it inside. The light shone on a smooth, dirt wall. The openings to three more caves were carved out of the dirt.

Matt was curious now. After all, they had come looking for an answer to his problem. He wasn't going to turn back now.

"I think we should go in," Matt said. "We might find what we're looking for."

"Maybe," Jason said. "But which way do we go?"

If Matt and Jason enter the first cave, go to page 12.

If Matt and Jason enter the second cave, go to page 56.

If Matt and Jason enter the third cave, go to page 96.

Continued from page 14

Monster. The word made Matt's blood run cold. His first instinct was to run, but he stopped himself.

He had come here looking for answers. Maybe this monster had them.

Jason turned and tried to climb back up the slippery slope. But Matt stepped forward.

"Do you know anything about this baseball bat?" he asked, taking the bat out of his backpack.

The monster made a low, gravelly sound. "Of course I know the bat. I created it. I am a Vashlock, after all," it said.

"A Vashlock?" Jason asked. "That sounds familiar."

"Vashlocks are wish-givers. We can give humans what they want," it said. It took a step closer, and Matt shuddered. "But now you have something *I* want. The bat. Have you come to return it to me?"

"N-n-not exactly," Matt said. He suddenly wished he had decided to turn and run instead.

"Then why are you here, then?" the monster asked. Its green eyes shone briefly, and then it nodded. "Ah, yes. You must be here to thank me. The bat has transformed you into a powerful hitter, hasn't it?"

"Yes," Matt said. That was true. "But there was a side effect." He pushed up his sleeve to show the monster the fur that was growing there.

The monster raised its three left arms and waved dismissively. "A minor side effect. Surely a little extra hair won't spoil the fact that you made it onto the Ravens?"

Matt was startled. "How did you know . . ." he started to ask, but then realized he didn't want an answer.

Jason had finally stopped trying to escape. He stood behind Matt, watching the monster carefully and brushing slime off his jeans.

The Vashlock slowly started to circle Matt and Jason, speaking slowly.

"You're very interesting, Matt," it said. "You're afraid of a little fur. But brave enough to find your way here to me. Very intriguing. You are just the sort of person who I like to do business with."

"Business?" Matt asked. Jason eyed the monster suspiciously.

The monster stopped circling and stood in front of Matt once more.

"I have a deal for you, Matt," it said. "How would you like to become the world's best baseball player? Because I can make that happen for you. That and so much more. And all you have to do is keep using your baseball bat."

"That's it?" Matt asked. It sounded too good to be true.

"I'll even make it easier," it said. "Just use the bat in three games. Just three. That's all."

Matt let the monster's words sink in.

"What do you get out of it?" he asked.

The Vashlock shrugged. "Fun. Amusement. I'm a wish-giver, remember? That's what Vashlocks do."

Matt thought some more. "What about the fur?" he asked.

The monster shook its head. "I'm disappointed in you, Matt. I didn't think you were the type of person to let a little fur stand in the way of greatness."

Matt had to admit that the monster made sense. The bat had clearly helped to make him better. Obviously, this Vashlock had some serious powers. Being the world's greatest baseball player had been Matt's dream since he could remember. Why not try it? What did he have to lose? The monster was right. He could stand a little fur.

"Don't trust it, Matt!" Jason hissed in his ear. "It's a monster!"

If Matt accepts the monster's offer, go to page 99.
If Matt refuses the monster's offer, go to page 90.

"We can't run for it," said Arnold. "They'll find us."

"Can somebody tell me what's going on here, anyway?" Matt asked.

"Your bat is more than a baseball bat," Arnold said. "It's a scientific breakthrough. A secret government agent stole it from its creator. Then we got word that they had lost the bat somehow. And then I saw you at the baseball field."

The sounds from the candy shop were getting louder. The men in blue would find the secret entrance any minute!

"Let's just give it to them," said the red-haired guy. "I'm tired of running and hiding."

Arnold sighed, and his shoulders slumped. "You might be right, Howdy."

"No way," Matt said. "We can run!"

The black-haired woman shook her head. "You don't know the S.R.A. There's no way to run from them."

"S.R.A.?" Matt asked.

"Onyx is talking about the Secret Recovery Agency," Arnold said. "They have resources we can't even dream of. Now that you've led them to our hideout, there's no point in running anymore."

Matt felt a twinge of guilt. It was his fault the S.R.A. had found Arnold's hideout. He reluctantly took the bat out of his pack.

"Okay," he said. "Let's give it to them."

Matt had barely finished the words when the two S.R.A. agents burst into the secret room. They immediately surrounded Matt and grabbed the bat.

Then Matt felt cold metal on his wrists. The agents were handcuffing him!

"Hey!" Matt cried. "I didn't do anything wrong!"

"You stole this device from a secret government laboratory," said one of the agents. "We don't know how you did it. But we'll find out."

During the commotion, Onyx and Howdy had fled out a back door. The other agent had handcuffed Arnold. Matt shot him a pleading look.

"Tell them, Arnold!" he cried. "Tell them I'm just a regular kid. I bought the bat in a junk shop!"

The agents snorted. "Junk shop," said one. "Very funny. Tell it to the secret judicial council you'll be facing."

The men hustled Matt and Arnold out into the street. Arnold leaned over and whispered in Matt's ear.

"Don't worry," he said. "Onyx and Howdy will

find us. They'll find some way to get us out."

Matt sighed. "I should have run for it when I had the chance," he muttered.

THE END

Continued from page 108

"Let's just keep the flashlight off for now," Matt said. "If we need it, we can use it."

Jason agreed. The two boys entered the cave, side by side. They found themselves in a narrow passageway.

"We can feel our way through," Matt whispered. He reached to the side to touch the wall. His fingers touched something cold and slimy.

Matt quickly pulled his hand away. The sticky mess oozed through his fingers. He wiped his hand on his jeans.

"Maybe not," he said.

They walked ahead, taking slow and careful steps. Then they hit a dead end. Matt grimaced and felt the walls once more, discovering that the passage turned to the left.

Once they made the turn, they saw a light flickering up ahead. They slowly approached.

The flickering light turned out to be a fire. Angel and Stan were tied up, sitting next to the flames.

The monster stood in front of them. Matt had never seen anything so horrible in his life. It had its back to them, but Matt could still see the brown, matted fur that covered its body. The monster wore a black loincloth, and two horns curved from the top of its massive head. The monster was shouting something at Angel and Stan.

"What now?" Matt whispered.

"We should attack it," Jason said.

"Good idea," Matt said sarcastically. "With what?"

Then, suddenly, Matt answered his own question. He remembered the bat in his backpack. He quietly removed it.

Then he turned to Jason and nodded.

"I'm going in," he said, trying to sound brave.

Matt snuck up behind the monster. He saw Angel's eyes widen in surprise, but Angel didn't give him away.

Matt closed his eyes. He was inches away now. He gripped the bat . . .

And then he swung.

The bat smacked against the monster's thick skull with a sickening sound. The monster swayed back and forth, then dropped to the ground. It looked like Matt had knocked it unconscious.

"Quick!" Stan shouted. "Untie us!"

Jason ran in, and the two boys untied Angel and Stan. The men used the ropes to quickly tie up the monster.

"It found out about our plan," Angel said as he

worked. "It didn't want to see the curse broken, so it captured both of us."

"That must mean that the plan will work!" Jason said excitedly. "We've got to hurry. The game's going to start soon!"

Go to page 132.

Continued from page 29

Matt decided to try to trick the Vashlock. He took a deep breath. "I've got a question for you," he said. "If you get it right, you win the challenge."

"Try me," said the monster.

"Okay," Matt said. He paused. "What's my name?"

The monster laughed. "Surely you can do better than that," it said. Its green eyes flickered for a few seconds. Then it smiled. "It's Matt, of course. Matt Carter. That's two out of three. I win!"

Matt shook his head. "Sorry. It's not Matt. It's Gabriel. You lose."

The monster frowned. "But the books in your backpack all say Matt. I looked right through it and saw them!"

Jason stepped up. "They do," he said. "But that's Matt's middle name. Gabriel is his real first name. I would have thought a powerful monster like you would know that."

The monster frowned. "Fine," it growled. "You win. But don't ever come back here again!"

The monster stomped its foot angrily. In the next second, Matt and Jason both found themselves on the hillside, outside the cave.

"Did that just really happen?" Jason asked warily.

"I think so," Matt said. "But I know one way to find out for sure."

Matt and Jason rode their bikes back to Bleaktown. Matt stopped in front of Sebastian Cream's Junk Shop. It was nighttime already, but the shop was open. Matt and Jason found Mr. Cream sweeping the floor inside.

He smiled when he saw them.

"Well, Matt," he said, "are you enjoying your bat?"

"Not exactly," Matt said. "A monster took it."

"Oh, I'm sorry to hear that," said Mr. Cream. "Can I interest you boys in anything else?"

Matt and Jason exchanged glances. Mr. Cream didn't seem bothered by the idea of a monster at all.

Matt thought about it. The bat had almost turned him into a furry beast. He and Jason had almost been captured by a monster.

"No, thanks!" Matt and Jason said together. Then they left the shop, jumped on their bikes, and headed home.

THE END

"Let's go back to the cave tomorrow," Jason said. "Maybe we can find out something more. If not, you can always play in the third game if you want."

That seemed reasonable enough to Matt. Jason wasn't asking him to give up just yet.

"Let's go after school tomorrow," Matt said. "There's no practice."

Jason gathered up his books. "I'm glad you're still listening to reason," he said. "I was worried you'd be halfway to beasthood by now."

"No way," Matt said, trying to laugh. He didn't want to tell Jason about the claws, or his new appetite. He wanted to see how things worked out tomorrow.

The next day, he and Jason biked to the Harding Hills after school. They found the cave entrance on the side of the hill. They entered and then went into the first cave entrance inside.

The last time he and Jason had taken that path, they had slid right into the monster's cave. Jason figured out a way they could avoid doing that.

"Last time, I counted out one hundred paces, remember?" he asked.

Matt nodded.

"Well, I'll count to ninety this time," he said. "Then we'll know to be on the lookout for the place when the path slides down."

Matt agreed, and Jason started counting. As soon as Jason reached the number ninety, they heard a sound. The boys stopped.

It was the Vashlock—and it was singing.

"Tricking boys is such a chore.
They're so boring, they make me snore.
That boy could break his deal with me.
If only he had eyes to see."

Matt strained to hear. The Vashlock was singing about him!

The monster continued the song.

"My name is Simon, that is true.
And if that boy knew what to do,
He'd use the bat in one more game.
Before the end, he'd say my name.
But Matt is not smart in the least.
And pretty soon, he'll be a beast!"

Matt felt Jason grab his arm. They ran back up the tunnel as quickly as they could and didn't stop until they reached the chilly night air.

"Did you hear that?" Jason said, catching his breath. "We know what to do now! We know how to break the deal!"

Go to page 118.

"Let's try the second cave," Jason said. "It looks bigger than the others."

Matt nodded. "You're right," he said. "Let's go."

The boys stepped through the cave entrance and found themselves in a narrow space. Jason's tiny light only reached a few feet ahead. So far, they couldn't see anything.

After about twenty yards, the cave opened in front of them into what looked like a large room. Jason slowly moved the light across the space.

To Matt's surprise, the light revealed furniture. There was a chair, a table, and even a shelf filled with books. Another shelf held cans of food.

"It looks like someone lives here," Matt whispered.

"Someone does live here," said a deep voice.

The boys jumped. Jason dropped his penlight, which clattered to the floor of the cave and rolled along the ground.

Matt found himself frozen with fear, his heart beating fast.

"Sorry," he said, his voice shaking. "We'll get out of here." He could hear Jason breathing quickly a few feet away.

"Not so fast," answered the deep voice.

Matt turned around. This was not a good situation. But without the light, he wasn't sure which way was out. He didn't want to run into whoever—or whatever—was in the cave with them.

The penlight stopped rolling. Matt followed the light, which shone on a pair of feet.

Huge, furry feet!

The feet shuffled to the side. Matt heard the sound of a match striking. Then an old-fashioned gas lantern lit up the cave.

A huge, hairy beast held the lantern. Brown fur covered its entire body. The dancing yellow lantern light illuminated its face: two pointy ears; a nose that looked like the snout of a dog or wolf; and two blue eyes, the only things that looked remotely human about the creature.

For a second, Matt was too stunned to move. But now that the cave was lit up, he could make out the exit. He grabbed Jason's arm and tore toward the hole in the wall.

"Wait!" cried the beast. "I'm not a monster! I'm Stan Cleaver!"

Matt kept running, but Jason stopped in his tracks.

"Stan Cleaver?" Matt heard Jason say behind him.

Matt turned. To his horror, he saw Jason

walking back into the beast's lair.

"Jason, no!" he cried.

"It's okay," Jason said. He stopped at the entrance, his eyes locked with the beast's. "Stan Cleaver used to play for the Hornets. He got recruited by the majors, but he disappeared right before spring training."

"How can he be Stan Cleaver?" Matt asked. "He looks like he *ate* Stan Cleaver."

"But I am Stan," the beast protested. "And if I was dangerous, I would have attacked you both by now, right?"

Matt admitted that made sense. But it didn't make him want to get any closer to Stan, or the beast, or whatever this hairy thing was.

"If you are Stan, prove it," Jason said. "What was your batting average in 1998?"

"Two-forty," the beast said. "Not one of my best years."

Jason's eyes narrowed. "And how many RBIs did you hit in 2000?"

"Um, fifty-seven, I think," the beast replied.

"Right both times. It's got to be Stan," Jason said, stepping closer. "What happened to you?"

"It's a long story," Stan sighed.

"Does it have anything to do with a baseball bat?" Jason asked.

The beast looked surprised. "How did you know?"

"Why don't you tell us your story, and we'll tell you ours," Jason said. "Right, Matt?"

"Uh, sure," Matt said hesitantly. In the light, he could see that the beast's fur looked pretty familiar—a lot like the stuff growing on his arms and legs. If this hairy guy used to be Stan Cleaver once, Matt figured he'd better find out how it happened.

Stan Cleaver sat in his chair and put the lantern on the table. Matt and Jason sat on the floor in front of him.

"I played in the minor leagues for six years," Stan Cleaver began. "For a local team. The Hornets."

"I know," Jason interrupted. "My dad owns them."

"Harry Hamilton?" said the beast. "Nice guy. It wasn't his fault I was unhappy. Playing for the Hornets was great, but I always wanted something more. Every year, the major-league scouts came around, and every year they passed me by."

Matt wondered how that would feel—to be so close to the majors, but to never get there.

"You might find this next part hard to believe," said Stan. He absently scratched his hairy back.

"Try us," Matt said.

"Well, I was hiking out here one day when I

came across a monster," Stan said. "An honest-to-goodness monster. It told me it was called a Vashlock, and it could grant wishes. It said it could make me a better baseball player—a player good enough to make the major leagues. It gave me a special bat. I started using it, and I was hitting great. So great that I got recruited. But there were . . . side effects."

Matt got a hollow feeling in his stomach. "Like growing fur?" he asked.

Stan nodded. "It was just some fuzz, at first. Then it got worse and worse. Pretty soon, I ended up looking like this. I've lived in this cave ever since." He sounded very sad.

Jason took the bat from Matt's backpack. "Did the bat look anything like this?" he asked.

Stan jumped to his feet. "That's it!" he cried. "I hope you kids aren't using it."

"I did already," Matt admitted. He pulled up his shirtsleeve.

Stan shook his head. "Stop using the bat, kid. You won't get any worse if you stop now. I promise."

Matt felt relieved. "Thanks," he said, standing up.

"Wait," Stan said. "Don't go! You're the first people I've talked to in years. Maybe you guys can help me."

"All I want to do right now is get rid of this

bat," Matt said. "I don't want to take any more chances." Matt raised the bat above his head. If he smashed the bat, it couldn't turn anyone into a beast ever again.

"Kid, don't do that!" Stan warned.

If Matt listens to Stan, go to page 74.

If Matt breaks the bat, go to page 123.

Continued from page 11

The metal bat won out. It just looked so cool. Matt put down the old wooden one.

"I'll take this one," he told Mr. Cream.

The shop owner nodded. Matt paid for the bat and quickly left the shop. He couldn't wait to try it out.

Matt headed right for the school field. The Ravens had just finished practice. Matt spotted his friend Jamal King. Jamal pitched for the Ravens.

"Hey, Jamal," Matt said. "Feel like pitching me a few? I just got a new bat I want to try out."

Jamal shrugged. "Sure," he said.

Matt stood at home plate and gripped the bat. It almost felt like it was humming beneath his fingers.

Jamal sent one over the plate. Matt swung the bat and hit a solid grounder that rolled right through Jamal's legs.

"I hit it!" Matt cried. He couldn't believe it.

"Not bad, Carter," Jamal said. "You been practicing?"

"I think it's the bat," Matt said. "Let's try again."

By now, some of the Ravens players had gathered around to watch. Matt spotted his best friend, Jason, on the side of the field. Jason didn't play baseball, but he loved the sport. He had probably stopped by the Ravens' practice to jot down statistics about the players.

Jamal pitched to Matt again. He hit the ball way out into left field this time. Jamal kept on pitching, and Matt hit almost every one.

Matt felt great. He had never been able to hit the ball before. This was definitely a lucky bat!

Matt was poised to bat again when he felt a hand on his shoulder. He looked up to see Coach Johnson.

"I didn't see you hitting like this in tryouts, Carter," he said. "You obviously had an off day. Why don't you show up for practice tomorrow? I think I can find a place for you on the team."

Matt felt like jumping for joy. But he played it cool. "Sure," he said. "I'll see you tomorrow!"

Go to page 71.

Continued from page 113

Matt was so startled that he handed over the bat without thinking. The man in blue nodded. Then he and his partner jumped into their car and sped away.

Matt stood, stunned, for a minute. The bat was gone! He couldn't hit without it. And just when he was about to make it big!

The next car to pull up was Matt's dad's. "Harry called my cell phone," he told Matt. "He wants to meet with us. I think he wants you to be on the team, Matt. Isn't that great!"

No, it's not great! Matt wanted to scream. *I don't deserve to be on the Hornets! The only reason I'm good is because of some weird bat!*

But Matt didn't say any of that. His dad looked so happy. Matt couldn't bring himself to disappoint him.

"Yeah, Dad," Matt said. "That's great."

Mr. Hamilton wanted to start Matt in a game that night. He had already told the local newspapers and TV stations that the Hornets would be unveiling a new star tonight.

"Once word gets out about you, we'll be selling tickets like crazy," Mr. Hamilton said cheerfully.

Matt tried to smile. "Uh, yeah," he said.

Mr. Hamilton had a Hornets uniform made up in Matt's size. He was all suited up, waiting for the game to start, when Jason found him in the locker room.

"Nice uniform," Jason said. "But where's the bat?"

"Gone," Matt said sadly. He explained what had happened outside the stadium.

"Wow, it sounds like a government conspiracy or something," Jason said. "Maybe Arnold was right."

Matt groaned. "I can't go out there! I'm going to strike out!"

"Maybe not," Jason said. "Maybe it wasn't the bat. Maybe you were good all along."

Jason's words gave Matt hope. When the game started, Matt ran out onto the field with the team. The crowd cheered.

Matt got up to bat in the first inning. He stood at the plate, waiting for the first pitch.

I was good all along, he told himself. *It wasn't the bat at all.*

The first pitch whizzed past his face.

"Strike one!" yelled the umpire.

Matt struck out on the next two pitches. The crowd booed and hissed.

Matt wanted to crawl under a rock. "I should have listened to Jason's cousin!" he moaned.

THE END

Continued from page 89

"I'm pretty sure it's left," Jason insisted.

Matt sighed. "Whatever. Let's go left."

They made a left turn. One block down, the street ended and branched off into a T shape. One turn led to a street Matt had never heard of. The other led to a dead end.

Matt shook his head. "I told you we should have made a right," he said. "Let's go back."

Matt and Jason turned around.

Then they stopped.

A hideous creature stood in the middle of the street, blocking their way. It towered above them. Brown, matted fur covered its body and it wore a black loincloth around its waist. Its strong, powerful arms ended in sharp-clawed hands.

But its face was worst of all. Huge, green eyes shone from hollows in its face. Two horns curved from the top if its head. And dozens of long, sharp teeth filled its huge, gaping mouth.

Monster. The word screamed in Matt's brain. This had to be the monster that had tricked Stan.

Matt tried to run, but his legs wouldn't move. He turned to look at Jason, who was frozen to the spot as well. Jason looked like he was going to pass out.

"There is no escaping my power," the monster growled. Its deep voice had an echo to it that made Matt's skin crawl.

"What do you want?" Matt asked, but he knew the answer.

The monster grinned. "I want my bat," it said. "Stan Cleaver thought he could get out of our deal. But he was wrong."

"I won't give it up," Matt said, surprising himself. "You tricked Stan. It's not fair."

Matt felt a surge of warm air, and in the next second, the monster was standing directly in front of him. Matt felt the monster's hot, sour breath on his face.

"You will give me the bat if you know what is good for you," the monster hissed.

Matt's small surge of bravery evaporated. He reached behind his back and pulled out the bat. Then he handed it to the monster.

The monster stepped back and smiled again.

"Remember, Matt," it said. "Nobody ever said life was fair."

Then a huge flame shot up in front of the monster. In the next instant, it vanished.

Matt found that he could move his legs again. He turned to Jason, who had collapsed to the street in fear.

"This is awful," Jason said. "Now Stan will

have to stay a beast forever."

Matt groaned. "I told you we should have turned right!"

THE END

Continued from page 103

Matt's claws creeped him out too much. He knew deep down that if he kept playing, things would only get worse. He'd probably grow hair over every inch of his body.

"Jason was right," Matt said to himself bitterly. "I never should have made a deal with a monster."

Matt wasn't sure how to break the news to Coach Johnson. If he started using a normal bat, the coach would see what a bad player he really was. He couldn't face that again.

So Matt decided to lay low for a while. The next day, he skipped practice, saying he didn't feel good. The day after that, the Ravens had a game against the Patriots, a team from a neighboring town. Matt faked a cold that morning and didn't go to school at all.

To Matt's relief, his mom let him stay home alone. He spent the day watching TV. The hours passed slowly. He wanted the day to be over. If everything went smoothly, he could relax a little.

Then Matt's digital clock read 4 p.m.—game time. He imagined the Ravens taking the field without him. Then he leaned back on his pillows as the clock clicked to 4:01.

He was about to close his eyes when a puff of

smoke exploded in his bedroom. The Vashlock stood there, waving away the smoke with all six of its hands.

"We made a deal, Matt," the monster said angrily. "Why aren't you playing in the game today?"

"The deal's off," Matt said, kicking his feet out from under the covers. "Claws were not part of our deal."

The monster's eyes flashed, and a cloud of darkness swept into the room. A cold chill crept into the air.

"A deal is a deal, Matt," growled the monster. "You broke our deal. And now . . . you must pay."

A scream erupted from Matt as the Vashlock lunged at him.

But no one heard him cry out.

THE END

Continued from pages 63, 78

Matt brought the metal bat to school with him the next day. He couldn't wait to try it out at practice. He just hoped it would work.

At lunch, he told Jason how he had gotten it.

"It's definitely an interesting bat," Jason said. "I've never heard of anything like it. And as you know, I'm something of an expert on baseball equipment."

You're an expert on everything, Matt thought, but he knew his friend wasn't bragging. There wasn't much Jason didn't know about baseball.

Jason agreed to come along with Matt to practice that afternoon. Practice started with jumping jacks, push-ups, sit-ups, and a jog around the field. Finally, Coach Johnson lined them up for batting practice.

Matt came up to the plate with his metal bat. Coach Johnson frowned. "That doesn't look regulation," he said.

Jason jumped off the bench and pulled a book from his pocket. "Actually, Coach, it meets the length and weight requirements. It shouldn't be a problem."

Coach Johnson grabbed the bat and peered at it closely. Then he shrugged. "Hmm, it looks like you're right. Go ahead, Matt."

Matt felt relieved. He just knew that if he had to use the team bat, he'd go back to being a no-hitter again. Then he wouldn't be on the team anymore.

Matt gripped the bat and tried to focus as Jamal sent a ball sailing over the plate. He swung, and hit a line drive past third base.

"Nice job," Coach Johnson called out, and Matt smiled for the first time since practice started. He caught his reflection in the metal bat. As long as he had the bat, everything would be fine.

Matt was still smiling when practice ended. He glanced up into the stands, imagining fans chanting his name when he played in the next Ravens game, when he noticed a strange figure sitting in the bleachers.

He was a tall man wearing a denim jacket. He wore his dark hair in dreadlocks down his back and a black beret on his head. He had a scruffy beard and wore sunglasses. And he seemed to be staring right at Matt.

Matt turned around, puzzled, and saw Jason walking up to him.

"I don't know what it is, but you really hit great today," Jason said. "It must have something to do with the bat."

"Yeah," Matt said. "Hey, did you see that strange guy in the stands?"

Jason suddenly looked surprised. "Oh, hey, Arnold."

Matt turned around. The man with dreadlocks

was standing right behind him.

"Hi, Jason," he said. "Is this kid here a friend of yours?"

Jason nodded. "Yeah, this is my friend Matt," he answered. "Matt, this is my cousin Arnold."

Arnold lowered his sunglasses and peered at Matt with his large, brown eyes. He raised his sunglasses again. Then he leaned toward them both and spoke in a whisper.

"You guys are in big trouble," he said. He slipped Jason a folded piece of paper. "Take this. Don't ignore it." Then he turned and swiftly walked away.

Jason shook his head. "Arnold's from the crazy side of the family," he said, opening the note. Then he read it aloud. *"Meet me at six a.m. at the Peanut Brittle Factory. Bring the bat."* The note gave an address, too.

Jason laughed. "Peanut Brittle Factory? I told you he was nuts."

Matt looked at the note. Then he looked at the bat.

Something weird was definitely going on. Maybe Arnold knew something about the bat. It was worth checking out.

If Matt checks out the Peanut Brittle Factory, go to page 81.

If Matt ignores the note, go to page 109.

Matt stopped. "Why not? Maybe breaking the bat will break whatever curse or spell is on us."

Stan shook his shaggy head. "I don't think so. I think I need the bat to get turned back to normal."

Jason looked curious. "What do you mean?" he asked.

Stan lumbered over to his shelf of books. He opened a book and came back holding a slip of paper.

"When the Vashlock gave me the bat, I found this inside the handle," he said. "It didn't make sense to me then. But I think it means something."

Stan read from the paper:

"To end the curse, an angel find,
And put him in a game.
And if a home run he can hit,
The beast will then be tame."

"I get it," Jason said. "If an angel hits a home run with the bat, then you'll be turned back to normal, right? *'The beast will then be tame.'* "

Matt frowned. "Are you kidding? How are we going to find an angel to hit a home run?"

"That's what I always wondered," Stan said glumly. "I mean, it's not like you can look up an angel in the yellow pages."

"How did you find the Vashlock?" Matt asked. "Did you look under 'M' for monster?"

"Very funny," Stan said. "This isn't helping, you know."

Matt looked to see if Jason had gotten the joke, but his friend's face was scrunched up in thought.

"Earth to Jason," Matt said. "Are you listening?"

Jason nodded. "I was thinking," he said, his face brightening. "What if the angel is a baseball player?"

Stan's eyes widened. "I never thought of that. Do you mean—"

"Angel Flores," Jason said. "He played in the majors for years, but he finished out his career with the Hornets."

"We played together," Stan said. "He's a good guy."

Matt shook his head. "So you think because his name is Angel, it will work the same way?"

Jason shrugged. "It's worth a try, isn't it?"

"I'll try anything," Stan said quickly.

Matt felt so confused. It was hard enough to believe they were talking to a hairy beast who used to be a baseball player. Would this whole

Angel thing really work? It seemed crazy.

"So what do we do now?" Matt asked, sighing.

"We find Angel Flores!" Jason exclaimed.

Go to page 86.

Continued from page 24

Matt got dressed, making sure to cover his arms and legs so no one would spot his mysterious brown fur. He jumped on his bike and headed for Sebastian Cream's shop. As he rode up to the entrance, Mr. Cream was just opening his door.

"Ah, young Matthew," Mr. Cream said, smiling. "Here to do some more shopping?"

Matt put the bat on the counter. "I'm here to complain about the bat," he said. He pushed up his sleeves. "See? It gave me this weird growth."

Mr. Cream shook his head. "Dear boy, didn't you read your receipt? I have a copy right here."

The little man took a piece of paper from inside the cash register and handed it to Matt. Matt saw a line of words in tiny print at the bottom. He squinted and Mr. Cream handed him a magnifying glass.

WARNING: This bat may cause the owner to temporarily turn into a hairy beast.

Matt couldn't believe his eyes. "Are you serious? That's crazy!"

Mr. Cream shrugged. "Nobody ever reads the fine print," he said. "The fur will disappear by the end of the day. But I'll give you back your money, of course. Unless . . ."

"Unless what?" Matt asked.

"Unless you would like to exchange it," Mr. Cream said. He pulled the metal bat from under the counter.

Matt looked at the metal bat. Even though the wooden bat had made him furry, it had gotten him a place on the Ravens. He didn't want to lose his place on the team. Maybe the metal bat would be a good luck bat, too.

Matt slowly took the bat. "Wait," he said. "Will this one turn me into a beast? Or a monster? Or anything else weird?"

"No," Mr. Cream said. He wrote out a new receipt and handed it to Matt. "I can guarantee that this bat will not turn you into any kind of creature."

"Fine," Matt said. "It better not, or I'll be back!"

Matt ran out of the store with his new bat. Mr. Cream shook his head.

"Nobody ever reads the fine print," he muttered.

Go to page 71.

Continued from page 29

"How about a catching contest?" Matt said, trying to sound confident. "I bet I can catch anything you can throw from ten yards away."

"Anything?" the monster asked.

"Sure," Matt said.

"Are you sure about this, Matt?" Jason asked nervously.

"It's the only thing I'm good at," Matt said. "I've got to try."

The monster nodded. It blinked, and suddenly it was dressed in a red baseball uniform. It wore a glove on one of its clawed right hands and held a baseball in one of its left hands. Matt discovered that a glove had appeared on his right hand, as well.

The monster's cave suddenly stretched out, so Matt and the monster were thirty feet apart.

"Ready?" the monster asked.

"Give it your best shot," Matt challenged.

The monster hurled the ball into the air. In the next instant, the baseball transformed into a spinning ball of fire.

"No way!" Matt cried.

The monster grinned. "You said you could catch *anything* I threw," it cackled.

Matt held out his glove . . . he had to try. But

at the last second, as the searing heat of the fire-ball came near him, he flinched. The ball fell to the ground, a normal baseball once more.

"Two out of three," said the monster. "I win. That means you lose!"

The monster blinked again. Matt and Jason suddenly found themselves in an underground chamber. Green slime oozed from the walls. Spiders skittered across the floor.

There were no doors or windows.

They were trapped!

"Sorry," Matt cried. "I guess I should have tried something else!"

THE END

"Maybe your cousin knows something about the bat," Matt said. "I think we should go."

Jason thought about it. "I'll see what my mom says," he suggested. "If she says it's cool, then we'll go."

Mrs. Hamilton seemed to think it was fine for the boys to meet Cousin Arnold, and laughed when Jason said Arnold was crazy. Matt awoke early the next morning and headed over to Jason's just before the sun rose over Bleaktown.

Matt and Jason looked at a map of town and then rode their bikes to the address Arnold gave them for the Peanut Brittle Factory. To Matt's surprise, he found it was a little shop on a street off of Main Street. It looked like an old-fashioned candy store. Jars of candy filled the windows.

Jason peered through the window. "It looks closed," he said.

Then Matt heard a sound. It was coming from the drainpipe. With a clatter, a red jelly bean rolled out of the bottom of the pipe and landed on the sidewalk. Matt picked it up.

"There's something written on it," he said. He squinted to read the writing.

GO TO THE BACK OF THE STORE.

Matt and Jason looked at each other and walked around to the back of the store. They found a door there. The lock of the door was small and round. Above it, engraved in the metal, were the words *INSERT JELLY BEAN HERE*.

Matt pushed the jellybean through the hole. Seconds later, the door opened.

Inside the candy shop, the boys found themselves in a dark room filled with computers and TV monitors. Cousin Arnold was sitting at a computer. He swung around and nodded when he saw Matt and Jason.

"Close the door behind you," he said.

Two other people sat at computer stations. One was a woman with short black hair and thick glasses with black frames. She wore a black turtleneck and black pants. The other was a tall, thin guy with bright red hair.

"This is Onyx," Arnold said, pointing to the girl. "And this is Howdy."

Onyx wheeled her chair right up to Matt and Jason. "Do you have the bat?"

"Yeah," Matt said, feeling too shocked to ask questions. He took the bat out of his backpack and held it toward her.

Howdy let out a low whistle. "You were right,

Arnold. It's a K-51, all right."

Jason snorted. "A K-51? I've never heard of any baseball bat with that name."

"That's because it isn't just any bat," Arnold said. "It's an important scientific discovery. So why don't you guys just hand it over to us? We know what to do with it."

Matt quickly redrew the bat. "No way. I need it," he said.

Arnold, Onyx, and Howdy looked at one another. Onyx and Howdy nodded. Arnold sighed and looked at the boys.

"I guess we'll have to tell you," he said. "Your bat is more than a baseball bat. It was developed in secret by a brilliant scientist named Leon Shingle. It may look like an ordinary baseball bat, but it actually has the ability to transport matter through time and space! When the government—"

"Hold on a second," Matt said. "Time and space? You've been reading way too much science fiction, dude."

Arnold shook his head. "I know what it sounds like. But you've got to believe us. Leon Shingle is one of the most brilliant scientists around. He's bigger than Einstein. Sharper than Hawking. That's why, when the government got wind of Shingle's invention, they sent the S.R.A. squad after it."

Matt snorted. Arnold's story was sounding more ridiculous by the second.

"The S.R.A. squad?" Jason asked.

"Secret Recovery Agency," Arnold said. "Nobody knows about them. They do the government's dirty work. They stole Shingle's bat."

"So how did Matt get it?" Jason asked. "I mean, it was just sitting there in Sebastian Cream's Junk Shop right out in the open. Right, Matt?"

Matt nodded.

Arnold shook his head. "We don't know. An alert went up two weeks ago that the bat had been stolen from the S.R.A. They think we took it."

"And who are *you*, exactly?" Matt asked, now even more confused.

"We call ourselves the Defenders of Justice," Arnold said. "We keep track of the S.R.A. and other secret organizations."

Matt took a step backwards. "You are definitely not convincing me. Defenders of Justice? Super secret organizations? How come we've never heard of you before?"

Onyx rolled her eyes. "Duh," she said. "Don't you know what *super secret* means?"

"You've got to trust us, Matt," Arnold said. "We've got a plan to protect the bat. But we need your help."

Matt had to think about it. Arnold and his friends looked very serious. But that had to be the craziest story he'd ever heard.

If Matt goes along with the plan, go to page 92.

If Matt decides to steer clear of the Defenders of Justice, go to page 136.

"We'll have to go at night," Stan said. "I can't go out during the day." He sadly looked at his furry body.

"Why do you even have to come?" Matt asked. "It might be safer if you stay here."

"I don't think Angel will believe us if Stan isn't there," Jason pointed out. "I mean, it's a pretty crazy story."

You can say that again, Matt thought. Stan knew where Angel lived, so the boys made a plan to meet him there around seven, when it got dark.

The boys biked back home. After dinner, Matt told his parents he was going to a movie with Jason. He went to Jason's house, and they walked over to the address Stan had given them.

The sky above was a deep shade of purple. They made turn after turn to get to Angel's block. Skinny, brick houses lined the street. Each one looked the same. They all had a clump of bushes next to the front door.

"I've never been in this part of Bleaktown before," Matt said.

"It's one of the older parts of town, I think," Jason said. "Anyway, I hope this is the right address."

They walked up the steps of house number fifty-nine. Matt looked around nervously for Stan.

"Stan," Jason whispered. "Are you here?"

But before they could get a reply, the front door opened. A tall man with dark hair stood there, frowning at them.

"What do you kids want?" he snapped.

"We're looking for you," Jason said. "You're Angel Flores, right?"

Angel's dark eyes narrowed in his deeply tanned face. "Are you looking for money or something? 'Cause I didn't make a bunch of money in the majors. That's what everyone thinks, but I didn't."

"Flores, when did you become such a grumpy old man?"

Matt jumped. It was Stan's voice. The hairy baseball player stepped out of the bushes. Angel gasped.

"What is this?" he asked. "Some kind of surprise TV show or something?"

"It's me, Stan Cleaver," Stan said.

Angel tried to focus his eyes in the darkness. "If that's you, Stan, then you need a haircut."

"It really is Stan, Mr. Flores," Jason said. "He's just a little . . . different."

Angel frowned again. "How do I know it's really him?"

"Let me think," Stan said thoughtfully. "How about this: I know that before every game you ate a peanut butter and bologna sandwich for good luck."

"That's right," Angel said. "But a lot of people know that."

"But they don't know that you always used Squirrelly Peanut Butter—super smooth, no chunks," Stan said. "And that you used to keep it in my locker."

Angel's eyes widened. Then he shook his head, stepping back.

"No way," he said, his voice shaking. "No way. This can't be real."

"It is real, Angel," Stan said softly. "Just let me explain."

Angel took a deep breath. "Okay. Come on inside."

They all sat down in Angel's living room. Jason and Stan took turns telling the story. Matt took the bat from his pack to show Angel.

"So you want me to hit a home run with this bat?" Angel asked when they were finished. "How is that supposed to work?"

"I had an idea," Jason said. "I could ask my dad to bring you back for a game. Sort of a special return from retirement."

"That could work," Angel said. "But there's no

guarantee I'll hit that home run. I'm a little rusty, you know."

"If anyone can do it, you can," Stan said. "Will you at least give it a try?"

Angel nodded. "It's crazy, I know. But you were always a good friend, Stan. I just can't say no."

It was late by the time they left Angel's house. Stan took off for his cave. Jason and Matt headed back home.

Jason talked the whole time about their plan. When Jason finally took a breath, Matt realized they had taken a wrong turn.

"I think we're lost," Matt said. "I don't remember turning down this street."

"Let's go to the corner," Jason said. "I think if we make a left, we'll be back on track."

They went to the end of the street and looked both ways. Matt had his doubts.

"I don't know," he said. "I think we should turn right."

If the boys turn left, go to page 66.
If the boys turn right, go to page 104.

Continued from page 44

Jason's words seemed to snap Matt out of a trance. Of course he couldn't make a deal with a monster. What was he thinking?

"Sorry," Matt said. "No deal. Just take back your bat."

The Vashlock's eyes flashed angrily. It grabbed the bat and snapped it in two.

"I don't like it when people refuse my generous deals," it growled. It slowly moved closer to Matt and Jason.

"Oh, no!" Jason cried. "It's going to eat us!"

The monster frowned. "That would be against the rules," it said. "But there must be something else I can do . . ."

Matt and Jason took a step back. The monster grinned. "I got it!" it said.

A blinding green light flashed from the monster's eyes. Matt's skin tingled as though a million tiny insects were crawling across his body.

The light faded. Matt looked at Jason. His friend was wearing a pair of pajamas that looked like a baseball uniform.

Matt looked down at himself and saw that he was wearing pajamas, too. His Christmas pajamas with a reindeer on the shirt. The reindeer's nose glowed in the dark.

"What's going on?" Matt wondered.

He and Jason weren't in the cave anymore. They were in a school bathroom. And not just any bathroom.

"The girls' bathroom," Jason whispered. "We've got to get out of here!"

But the school bell rang. The bathroom door opened, and a group of sixth-grade girls walked in. They screamed when they saw Matt and Jason. Then they burst out laughing.

Matt turned to Jason. "The next time we see a monster," he said, "remind me to run away!"

THE END

Continued from page 85

Matt thought about it. Arnold and his friends were weird, but they seemed pretty serious. Besides, he knew the bat wasn't an ordinary bat. He was anxious to find out more about it.

"All right," Matt said. "I'll help you. What's the plan?"

Arnold reached under a table and pulled out what looked like an instrument case. When he opened it up, it revealed a bat that looked just like Matt's.

"The S.R.A. must know you have the K-51 by now," he said. "But we have an advantage. They don't know that we've contacted you. Use this duplicate bat at your next practice. Since the S.R.A. knows that you have the bat, they're going to show up at practice tomorrow to take it. That will give us time to get the K-51 back to Dr. Shingle."

Arnold handed the duplicate bat to Matt. He hesitated. If he turned in the K-51, he'd stop being a power hitter.

But deep down, he knew it was the right thing to do. The bat didn't really belong to him. It belonged to this Leon Shingle guy.

"Okay," Matt said, sighing. He handed Arnold

the bat. Then he took the duplicate and put it in his backpack.

"Thanks, Matt," Arnold said. "Dr. Shingle will be so grateful."

"Yeah," Matt tried to smile, but he was worried. How was he going to play on the Ravens now?

The next day, Matt took the duplicate bat to practice, but he didn't even get to try it out. As soon as he got up to the plate, a black car came screeching up next to the field. Two men in blue uniforms got out. They ran up to home plate, grabbed the bat from Matt, and ran back to the car.

"Hey! What are you guys doing?" Coach Johnson yelled. He blew the whistle around his neck.

The car sped off, and Coach Johnson came back to the field, shaking his head. "I've got to call the police," he said. "Sorry, guys. No practice today."

Jason gave Matt a knowing look from the side-lines. It had happened just like Arnold had said it would.

"I guess your cousin was right," Matt said as they walked home together. Still, he didn't feel very happy. There would be another practice tomorrow, and Coach Johnson would find out he couldn't hit, after all.

Matt said good-bye to Jason. When he got home, he found a long, thin package outside his front door. He read the label. It was addressed to him!

Matt took the package up to his room. He closed the door behind him and tore the brown paper off the package. Then he ripped open the box underneath.

Inside the box was a bat. It looked just like every other bat used in his baseball league. He lifted up the bat, and a note slid onto his lap. Matt opened it up and read it.

Dear Mr. Carter:

Arnold tells me what a help you were in retrieving the K-51. I am forever in your debt. I have enclosed a replacement bat. It's ergonomically designed to give you precision batting power. Unlike the K-51, it does not have the ability to transport matter through time and space, but I think you'll find it does a good job on the baseball field.

Sincerely,

Dr. Leon Shingle

Matt turned the bat around in his hands and grinned. He couldn't wait to try out his new bat tomorrow.

He had a feeling about this one.

THE END

Continued from page 40

"Three is my lucky number," Matt said. "Let's try the third cave."

Jason shrugged. "Might as well."

The boys stepped through the cave entrance. Jason shone his pocket flashlight around. They were in a small cave with a low, curved ceiling. Matt jumped as something skittered across the beam of light. Then he let out a sigh of relief—it was just a bug.

Jason examined the walls carefully, looking for some kind of clue. But there was nothing.

"Let's try the other caves," Jason suggested.

They turned back toward the cave entrance. Suddenly, a strange, cackling noise filled the air. It sent a chill down Matt's spine.

Then another noise replaced it. A noise like rolling thunder. At the same time, Matt saw a dark shadow headed toward the cave opening.

In an instant, Matt realized what was happening. Something was heading toward the cave's entrance! He grabbed Jason's arm and pulled him toward the opening.

But before they escaped, the ground began to shake violently underneath them, sending them both sprawling to the ground. Seconds later, a huge boulder slammed against the opening of the cave.

"No!" Matt cried. He jumped up and ran to the boulder, pushing at the heavy rock with all his might.

Jason got up and did the same. Even with both of their strength, the rock wouldn't budge.

"We're trapped," Jason announced, his voice filled with panic. "Probably some kids blocked us in. I bet that's what that laughing was about." Jason began to pound on the rock with his fists, and scream for help.

Matt doubted that the evil laugh came from a bunch of kids, but he didn't want to scare Jason. There had to be a way out of this. He reached into his backpack and took out his cell phone. No service.

"Of course," Matt muttered bitterly. "Why would there be service the one time I really need it!"

Jason finally stopped screaming. "Maybe some-one will pass by in the morning," he said, his voice hoarse. "We might as well settle in for the night."

"I guess," Matt said. "But I'm not going to fall asleep in this place."

"Me, neither," Jason agreed.

Matt kept thinking about how worried his par-ents must be. That kept him awake for a while. So did the itching on his furry arms and legs, which seemed to get worse every minute.

Jason stayed awake by reciting the batting averages of every major-league baseball player, in alphabetical order. But after a while, Jason's penlight died out, and Matt felt his eyelids droop.

When Matt opened his eyes again, he could see clearly, even though the cave was still pitch-black. He saw his clothes in a heap on the floor next to him. Puzzled, he looked down at his body.

Brown fur covered every inch of his body! He reached up to feel his face and saw that his fingernails had become long, black claws. He felt the fur sprouting all over his face, and discovered that his nose had grown, too. It felt cold and wet, like a dog's nose. And he must have been able to see in the dark because of his monster vision!

But to his surprise, Matt didn't seem bothered by this at all. He felt good. Strong.

On the ground, a sleeping figure began to stir. In the back of Matt's mind, he knew this was Jason, his friend. But Matt didn't feel like Matt anymore. He felt like a beast. And to the beast, Jason didn't look like Jason anymore . . .

He looked like breakfast!

THE END

Continued from page 44

But Matt ignored Jason. The Vashlock's deal sounded too good to be true. He wanted to keep playing for the Ravens. He wanted to become the best player in the world. So why couldn't he use the monster's bat? After all, he had bought it, fair and square.

"I'll do it," Matt said.

The monster grinned. "Of course you will," it said.

Matt didn't like the tone in the monster's voice, but it was too late to change his mind now. He was determined to be the best baseball player in the world.

Suddenly, the Vashlock turned away from them, as though it was finished with them.

"Uh, Mr. Vashlock?" Jason asked in a squeaky voice. "How are we supposed to get out of here?"

The monster turned around and sighed. "I suppose I have to do everything for you, don't I?"

A bright green light shone from the monster's eyes. Matt's skin tingled, as though it was crawling with a million tiny insects.

The green light died down. To Matt's surprise, he discovered that he wasn't in the cave anymore. He was home in his room, in his bed. Matt lifted up the covers and saw he was wearing his pajamas. The bat was propped up against his pillows.

Matt jumped out of bed, his heart pounding. What had just happened? Was it real? Then he heard his cell phone ring. Matt switched on his light and fished the phone out of his backpack.

It was Jason. "Matt, are you all right? Did you end up at home, too?"

"Yeah," Matt said. "The monster must have done it."

"This is too weird, Matt," Jason said. "You should take that bat tomorrow and throw it off a cliff or something. Forget all about that monster. We shouldn't be messing around with it."

Matt felt suddenly annoyed. Of course Jason would chicken out. He just didn't understand. Jason loved numbers and statistics and stuff, and he was good at it. Matt loved baseball, but he wasn't good at it—until now. He wasn't going to give that up.

"I'll talk to you tomorrow, okay?" Matt said. Then he hung up without waiting for Jason's answer.

The next day was Sunday. Matt avoided answering Jason's phone calls. Instead, he got his dad to take him to the ball field so he could practice his hitting. Matt's dad pitched ball after ball, and Matt hit almost all of them.

"I'm proud of you, Matt," his dad had said on the drive home. "You must have really practiced hard to get this good."

Matt felt a little twinge of guilt—but just a little one.

The next day, after school, the Ravens played their first game. Coach Johnson made Matt sit on the bench for the first few innings.

"You haven't been to enough practices yet," he said. "I'll bring you in when I need you."

Matt glared at the coach from the bench. It was his first game, and he wasn't even going to get to play!

Matt watched the game with his chin in his hands. Then, at the bottom of the third inning, he heard a cry from the field.

Evan Rogers, an outfielder, was hopping around on one leg, grabbing his ankle. Evan had just been rounding third base.

"I think I sprained my ankle or something," Evan told Coach Johnson. He tried to step on it, but winced in pain. A medic ran off the sidelines with an ice pack and helped Evan to the bench.

Coach Johnson looked at Matt. "Looks like you're in," he told him.

Matt jumped off the bench. Sure, he felt bad about Evan, but that wasn't his fault.

Or maybe it is, a little voice in his head said. It

sounded like Jason. *Maybe it has something to do with that monster.*

Matt quickly pushed the thought aside. He ran out into the outfield to join his team.

In the seventh inning, Matt finally got his chance at bat. Jamal King, the Ravens' pitcher, was on second base.

"Heads up, Jamal," Matt called out. "I'm going to bring you home."

The Ravens on the bench laughed and shook their heads.

"Prove it, Carter!" one of them called out.

Matt didn't hesitate. When the pitcher drove the ball across the plate, he pounded it into the outfield. Jamal ran home easily, and Matt rounded the bases, too. He had hit a home run on his first try!

The Ravens went wild. Matt's home run had put them way in the lead.

"Good job, Carter," Coach Johnson said. "You'll be starting next game."

Matt ran all the way home. He couldn't wait to tell Jason what had happened—

Then he changed his mind. Jason would only give him a hard time about the monster. No, he'd just tell his mom and dad. They'd probably take him out for pizza again.

Matt ran upstairs and pulled off his baseball

cleats. He tore off his socks and stifled a scream. His toenails had turned into long, black claws. Long, thick fur covered his feet.

This was more than just a little fur. Matt started to panic. What was happening to him?

Matt picked up the bat and stared at it. "Just use the bat to play three games," the monster had said. Matt had played one game so far. Maybe he should stop now. If he stopped, nothing worse could happen, right?

If Matt decides not to use the bat in the second game, go to page 69.

If Matt goes ahead and uses the bat in the second game, go to page 125.

Continued from page 89

Matt and Jason made a right turn. They soon found themselves on a familiar street.

"Thank goodness," Matt said. "I have to head home before my mom kills me."

"Let's talk to my dad tomorrow," Jason said. "I'm sure he'll go for it."

The next day, they made up a story for Mr. Hamilton about how Angel wanted to make a comeback—leaving out the part about Stan Cleaver and the monster. Thankfully, Mr. Hamilton thought it was a great idea.

"Angel Flores was always one of our most popular players," he said. "He really knew how to charm the fans. I'm sure they'd love to see him back. He can play in a couple of weeks."

"Can't you do it sooner?" Jason asked. He was anxious to see if the whole thing would work.

But Mr. Hamilton insisted on enough time to publicize the game. He called up Angel and asked him to play in a home game in two weeks.

"That's all right," Matt reasoned. "I bet Angel needs time to practice anyway."

Matt was right. Angel might have seemed calm when he agreed to help them, but he got nervous once the date was set. He went to the Hornets' stadium every day to practice. When Matt wasn't practicing with the school team, he and Jason went to the stadium to see Angel.

Matt was glad for the break. He had stopped using the wooden bat to keep from becoming a beast, which meant he had pretty much gone back to his old way of hitting. Coach Johnson wasn't happy, but he kept Matt on the team. He just never let him play.

"Hey, Matt," Angel called up to the bleachers. "Why don't you come down here and help me?"

Matt was thrilled. He started by hanging out in the outfield, going after balls that Angel hit.

"You're pretty good, Matt," Angel remarked. "What made you use that cursed bat in the first place?"

Matt sighed. It embarrassed him to talk about his batting problems—especially with a former pro like Angel.

Jason solved the problem for him. "He can't hit!" he yelled from the sidelines.

"Of course you can hit. Anyone can hit," Angel said.

Matt shook his head. "You haven't seen me yet. Jason's right."

"We'll see about that." He handed Matt his practice bat. "Let's see what you can do."

Angel watched as one of the Hornets pitched a

few balls to Matt. He missed each one. Then Angel walked up to Matt.

"You just need some confidence," he said, "and maybe a little help with your stance."

Angel placed Matt's feet so that his back foot was closer to the base than his front foot.

"You were using a closed stance," he said. "Most players do. But you have trouble moving your hips right. I know, 'cause I do, too. This way, your hips open automatically. You'll have a better view of the pitcher, too."

Matt took a swing at the air. He liked the way he felt.

"Just make sure not to pull away from the pitch," Angel advised him. "Stay steady."

Matt nodded. The Hornets' pitcher lobbed an easy one into him, and he made contact. The ball soared into right field.

"Not bad, Matt," Angel said. "I think you'll get the hang of it."

Over the next two weeks, Angel kept practicing, and Matt got more batting tips from Angel. He couldn't remember having a better two weeks his whole life.

Finally, the night of the big game arrived. Matt and Jason headed to the cave to see Stan. Stan was planning on attending and sitting in the stands. Jason had gotten him a disguise—a long, beige trench coat and a cowboy hat.

"What do you think?" Stan asked, obviously pleased. "I look pretty good, huh?"

"Uh, sure," Matt said, not wanting to hurt his feelings. In that getup, Stan looked more weird than ever. But at least it covered his fur.

Then Matt and Jason headed to Angel's house to give him the bat. Jason rang the doorbell, but Angel didn't come to the door. Jason rang the bell again.

"That's weird," Matt said. He gently pushed on the door, and it swung open.

"Uh-oh," Matt said.

Angel's house was a wreck. Furniture was knocked over and Angel's trophies were piled on the floor. Jason bent down and picked up a sandwich from the mess.

"Peanut butter and bologna," he said solemnly.

They searched the house for Angel, but couldn't find him.

"I have a bad feeling about this," Jason said. "Maybe we should go back to see Stan."

Matt nodded. They hopped on their bikes and headed back to the hills. The game was scheduled to start in two hours, but that was the last thing Matt was worried about. He just hoped that Angel was all right.

When they got to Stan's cave, they found it had been wrecked, too. Matt saw Stan's cowboy hat on the floor, as though someone had stepped on it. He frowned. Something was definitely wrong.

"Do you think they're . . . alive?" Matt asked slowly. He kept thinking about the monster that had given Stan the bat. Monsters, generally, weren't too nice.

"I don't know," Jason said. "But there's no blood or anything. That's a good sign."

Jason looked around. Then he pointed to something. "Look!" he said. "Scuff marks. In the dirt. Like something was dragged out of here."

Matt saw Jason was right. The scuff marks were easy to make out on the dusty cave floor. They followed the marks outside the cave. They led to one of the other caves carved into the hill—the first one Matt and Jason had seen.

Jason reached into his backpack and pulled out a flashlight.

"Come on," he said.

But Matt stopped him. "Maybe we shouldn't use that," he said. "If something in there has Angel and Stan, we don't want it to see us coming."

"But if we can't see where we're going, we'll never find them," Jason argued.

If Matt and Jason don't use the flashlight, go to page 48.
If Matt and Jason use the flashlight, go to page 114.

Continued from page 73

Then Matt realized how silly he sounded. Peanut Brittle Factory? Six a.m.? All he needed to know about the bat was that it made him a good hitter. He didn't want to know any more.

Matt took the note from Jason, crumpled it up, and stuffed it into his pocket. "No offense, but I've got better things to do than hang around a nut factory with your cousin," Matt said.

Jason shrugged. "I don't care. I won't see him until Thanksgiving, anyway. Last year, he wouldn't let us eat any of the sweet potatoes because he said they were the result of a secret government experiment."

"That is pretty strange," Matt admitted.

By the next practice, Matt had forgotten all about Jason's cousin. Matt did so well in practice that Coach Johnson asked him to bat fourth in their next game against the Patriots.

Matt's mom, dad, and sister Kayla came to see his first game. Jason came with his father, too. Even though Jason's dad, Mr. Hamilton, owned a minor-league team, he hated to miss a good local game.

Matt didn't disappoint his family and friends.

He hit a double on his first try at bat. He ran in four batters by the time the game was over, leading the Ravens to a victory of 9-2 over the Patriots.

Matt's family went out to celebrate with Jason and his dad. Everyone talked about the game as they ate their pizza, but Matt's mind wandered.

The bat had felt strange in his hands all through the game. He had felt that buzzing again, and he could almost swear he heard it hum when he used it. Whatever success he had today was because of the bat—not because of him.

"Keep it up, Matt," Mr. Hamilton said as he reached for a slice of pepperoni pizza. "I just might recruit you for the Hornets. We could use a good power hitter."

"That's my boy," Matt's dad said, ruffling Matt's hair.

Mr. Hamilton has to be joking, Matt thought. No kid his age had ever played on a minor-league team. But it was a great compliment. Matt should have been happy, but he knew it was the bat that was making him hit well. Without it, he'd still be a no-hitter.

Still, Matt kept using the bat. And he kept getting better and better. He hit two home runs in his next game. He followed that up by batting in five runs in one game. Within a week, the *Bleaktown News* ran a story about Matt on the front page of the sports section.

"Ravens' New Power Hitter Propels Team to the Pennant," the headline read. Matt's teammates teased him about it, but they were too happy to be winning to be jealous.

"Keep this up, and we'll win the state championship," Coach Johnson told him proudly.

After the article came out, people from all over Bleaktown came to see the Ravens' games to get a look at Matt in action. About a week later, Mr. Hamilton came over to talk to Matt and his parents.

"I know I made a joke about this before," he was saying. "But Matt's a good, solid player. He's packing people in the stands here in Bleaktown. I think he'd be a great asset to the Hornets."

Matt couldn't believe his ears. "You want mc to play for you? But that's the minors!"

"You're good enough, Matt," Mr. Hamilton said. "I've never seen anyone hit like you before. And people are already packing the bleachers to see you."

"As long as it wouldn't interfere with his schoolwork," Matt's mom said cautiously.

"I promise it won't," Mr. Hamilton said. "But I tell you what. Let me at least bring Matt in for a practice against my guys. We'll see if he can handle it."

Matt's dad turned to him. "What do you think?"

Matt forgot all about the bat. He was being given a chance to play with the minors! That was one step away from the big leagues. "Wow!" Matt exclaimed.

So Matt went to a practice session with the Hornets the next Saturday. Everything went great. Matt hit just about everything the pitcher delivered. The Hornets didn't look thrilled about it, but he could tell they were pretty impressed.

After the practice, Matt stood outside the Hornets' stadium, swinging his bat in the sunlight. His dad would be here to pick him up any minute. Mr. Hamilton wanted to talk to him. He was sure it was about Matt joining the Hornets. He couldn't believe his luck. *Boy, am I glad I stopped in Sebastian Cream's Junk Shop,* Matt thought to himself. *If I didn't, none of this would have ever happened!*

Suddenly, a black car screeched to a stop in front of the stadium. Two men in blue uniforms got out. They wore blue baseball caps pulled over their eyes, so Matt couldn't make out their faces.

"That bat does not belong to you," one of the men said. "Please hand it over right now."

If Matt hands over the bat, go to page 64.

If Matt escapes with the bat, go to page 15.

Continued from page 108

"All right," Matt said reluctantly. "We'll use the flashlight."

Matt and Jason entered the cave and found themselves in a narrow passageway. Green slime the color of lima beans oozed down the walls. *It kind of smells like lima beans, too*, Matt thought to himself. He shuddered.

The path veered to the left. As soon as they made the turn, Jason's flashlight revealed an amazing scene.

Just ahead, Angel and Stan sat on the ground next to a fire, tied tightly in ropes. A creature stood in front of them—a huge, muscular creature covered in matted brown fur. It wore a loincloth made of ratty black fur, and two horns curved from the top of its head.

"The monster," Matt whispered. "It has to be."

Suddenly, the monster turned around. Its face looked like something out of a nightmare. Green eyes glowed in its face. Two huge nostrils flared in its black, pig-like nose. Razor-sharp teeth filled its wide mouth.

Pure, unleaded fear flowed through Matt's veins. The monster looked at them and snarled.

"Kill the flashlight!" Matt barely managed to

get out the words. "It gave us away!"

But it was too late. The monster charged at them.

Instinct took over. Matt reached for the only weapon he had—the bat in his backpack. He pulled it out and swung at the monster with all his might.

The monster ducked. Matt swung again.

At the same time, Jason dodged right past them. He started to untie Angel.

The monster had Matt backed into a corner. Matt kept swinging the bat, but the monster kept getting closer.

Then he heard Angel's voice. "Leave him alone!"

The monster swung around. Angel charged at him. But the monster picked him up by the waist and threw him back into the cave. He landed on the floor with a thud.

The monster turned back to Matt again. "You're starting to annoy me," it growled in a voice that turned Matt's knees to jelly.

Then, suddenly, the monster sank to the floor. Stan stood over him, holding one of the logs from the fire.

"I've been wanting to do that for a while," he said, grinning.

Stan tied up the monster. Matt ran to Angel,

who wore a pained look on his face. He was sitting up and cradling his arm.

"I think it's broken," he said through gritted teeth.

Matt lifted Angel up by his good arm. "Come on," he said. "We've got to get out of here."

Stan had an old van hidden nearby that he kept so he could drive around at night, when no one could see his fur. He recovered his disguise from his cave and then helped Matt and Jason load Angel into the van.

"We're taking you to a hospital," he said.

"I'm sorry," Angel said sadly. "I guess I won't be hitting that home run now."

"How did you guys get back there?" Jason asked.

"The monster found out what we were up to," Stan said. "It didn't want us to break the curse, so it captured me and Angel."

Jason looked thoughtful. "So that means it would have worked," he said. "Even though you're not a real angel."

Angel nodded.

Jason's eyes traveled to Matt's backpack. His mom had ordered it for him. It was embroidered with his initials: GMC. Jason grew quiet for a moment and then his eyes lit up.

"Wait a second!" he exclaimed. "Matt, that G

stands for Gabriel, right?" he asked.

Matt nodded. "Yeah. You know. It's my real first name."

Angel suddenly smiled through the pain. "I get it! Matt can take my place."

Matt couldn't believe what he had heard. "What are you talking about?"

"Gabriel is the name of an angel," Angel said. "And not just any angel. He's a major angel. And that makes you an angel, too. So all you have to do is hit a home run, and the curse will break!"

Matt's head was spinning. "No way!" he exclaimed. "I can't hit a home run in a minor-league game."

"And it won't be easy convincing my dad to let Matt play in a minor-league game," Jason pointed out. "Why can't we just wait until Angel is better?"

Stan shook his head. "No use. Back in the cave, the Vashlock told me that the loophole runs out tonight. If an angel doesn't hit a home run by midnight tonight, then I'm stuck like this forever," he said sadly.

Go to page 138.

"How exactly do we break the deal?" Matt asked. The monster's song had sounded like a silly rhyme to him.

Jason put a finger to his lips. "Better go outside," he said. "I don't want the Vashlock to hear us."

The boys walked back out of the cavern.

"All right," Matt said, anxious for the whole ordeal to be over. "Tell me!"

"The monster told us in the song," Jason said. "In the first verse, it sang, '*That boy could break his deal with me. If only he had eyes to see.*' "

"Okay," Matt said. "Got it so far."

"It told us how with the second verse," Jason continued. " '*If that boy knew what to do, he'd use the bat in one more game. Before the end, he'd say my name.*' "

Matt looked at Jason blankly. He still didn't understand.

Jason sighed. "Don't you get it? The boy is you. You have to play in the third game. But before the game is over, you have to say the monster's name."

Matt suddenly understood. "Now I get it!" he exclaimed. "The monster's name is Simon, right? That's what it said in the song."

Jason nodded. "Let's just hope it works."

Matt looked at the cave opening. "You don't

think the Vashlock heard us, do you?"

Jason grabbed his backpack. "Let's not stick around to find out. If it finds out we're on to it, it might try to end the deal—some other way."

Matt remembered the monster's sharp claws and long, pointed teeth and shuddered.

The next game wasn't until after the weekend. Matt spent every spare minute checking his skin to make sure he wasn't sprouting any more fur. But that seemed to have stopped for now. He still couldn't get enough meat, though. In two days, he ate three platefuls of roast beef, two barbecued chickens, six hamburgers, and four pork chops.

By the time the game rolled around on Monday, Matt was nervous. The Ravens were playing a team from Smithville called the Pirates. The stands were filled with cheering fans who had come to see Matt play. But he didn't notice any of them. He just kept thinking about Jason's plan.

Would it work? There was only one way to find out. Matt would have to play in the game.

Because Matt's concentration was off, his hitting wasn't as spectacular as it had been, but it was still pretty good. He got on base twice, but didn't drive in any runs. By the time the ninth inning rolled around, the Ravens and Pirates were tied, 3-3.

Matt got up to bat in the bottom of the ninth. The bases were empty, and the Ravens had two outs. Matt didn't want the game to go into extra innings. He wanted the game to be over—now.

Matt walked to the plate, trying to keep his focus. But he saw something in the stands from the corner of his eye. Matt looked up to see the Vashlock on the very highest bleacher.

The monster grinned, revealing every one of its sharp teeth. It waved a pom-pom in one of its huge claws.

It doesn't know, Matt realized, suddenly feeling confident. *It thinks it's here to watch me turn into a beast. Well, I've got a surprise for it!*

Matt focused his attention on the pitcher. He lobbed the ball across the plate, and Matt swung with all his might. The ball soared over the pitcher's head, over the outfield, and over the fence!

"Home run!" the umpire yelled.

The crowd cheered as Matt rounded the bases, but Matt didn't hear any of it. As soon as he touched home plate, the game would be over.

Matt looked up into the bleachers. The Vashlock was on its feet now, smiling more broadly than ever.

Matt stopped right before touching home plate. He took a deep breath, waved up at the monster, and called, "Hi, Simon!"

The monster's smile turned to a scowl. It angrily

stomped its foot on the bleachers.

Then there was a puff of smoke, and it was gone.

Matt stepped onto home plate, and the rest of the Ravens surrounded him, cheering. He broke through his teammates to find Jason running toward him from the sidelines.

"Did it work?" Jason asked.

Matt pushed up his shirt sleeve. The fur on his arm had gone. He quickly kicked off one of his cleats and pulled off his sock. His foot looked like a normal foot again.

"We did it!" Matt said, relief sweeping over his body. "Thanks, Jason. I'm glad I listened to you."

"I can't believe this all started when you bought that bat," Jason said. "What are you going to do with it?"

Matt looked at home plate, where he had left the bat after hitting the home run. It wasn't there.

"Maybe it vanished, too," Matt said. "Just like the fur did."

No more bat meant no more being a star baseball player, Matt knew. But he was so relieved not to turn into a beast that it didn't seem so important anymore.

"We should celebrate," Jason said.

"Yeah," Matt agreed. But there was something else he wanted to do, too.

This whole weird adventure had started at

Sebastian Cream's Junk Shop. He wondered what other things he might find if he went back there.

Go to page 143.

But Matt didn't listen to Stan. He brought the bat down with all his might, smashing it against a rock sticking out of the ground.

There was a sickening sound as the bat exploded into a thousand splinters. Stan watched the bat in horror.

Steam began to rise from Stan's fur with a loud hiss. In the next instant, the steam exploded into a cloud, vaporizing Stan right in front of their eyes.

"What happened?" Matt asked, stunned.

Jason knelt down and picked up a splinter from the bat!

"The curse must have connected Stan and the bat somehow," Jason guessed. "When you destroyed the bat, you must have destroyed Stan."

"Oh, no!" Matt wailed. He felt terrible. "I should have listened when Stan said not to break the bat!"

Matt pushed up his sleeve. All of the fur had disappeared.

"So I guess it's over," Matt said sadly.

"Yeah." Jason nodded solemnly.

The two boys left the cave. Matt looked back over his shoulder. He was glad to get rid of his fur, but something bugged him.

"I wish I hadn't smashed that bat," he muttered. "I bet there was a way we could have helped Stan."

THE END

Continued from page 103

"It's nothing," Matt told himself. He remembered how it felt to hit that home run, to hear the crowd cheering. He wasn't about to give that up. Not because of a few gnarly toenails.

Matt took a shower and got dressed, putting a pair of heavy socks on his feet. The black claws poked through the cotton. Matt frowned and put on his sneakers. If he didn't have to look at his feet, he wouldn't have to think about them.

Matt went downstairs. His mom and dad had come home from work. He told them all about hitting the home run.

"Way to go, Matt!" Mrs. Carter said, giving him a big hug. "I knew you could do it!"

"This calls for pizza!" Mr. Carter said.

Normally, Matt would have been happy. But the thought of just tomato sauce and cheese didn't sound so appealing anymore. He was craving more than pizza.

"How about the Burger Barn?" Matt asked. "I could go for a juicy meat patty. Or two. Or three." The thought of the meat made his mouth water.

Matt's mom laughed and shook her head. "I forget that I've got a growing boy on my hands.

Burger Barn it is!"

Matt didn't eat three burgers at Burger Barn—he ate four. His parents laughed and attributed it to all the exercise he was getting.

All during dinner, a little warning clicked in Matt's mind.

This isn't like you, Matt, the voice said. *Something's happening to you. You're changing.*

But Matt pushed the thoughts aside.

Just two more games, he told himself. *Two more games, and you'll be the best baseball player in the world.*

That night, Matt had a hard time getting to sleep. His stomach made strange, gurgling noises.

Must be all those burgers, Matt thought. *I'm not doing that again.*

Matt closed his eyes and began to count sheep, just like his mom had taught him to do when he was little. First, he imagined a little white fence sitting on top of a green hill, with a sunny blue sky in the background.

Then the first fluffy white sheep came bounding up to the fence. It jumped over, happily kicking its legs in the air.

One, Matt counted.

Then the second sheep came, soaring over the fence like an Olympic pole-vaulter.

Two, Matt counted.

Then the third sheep ran toward the fence. But the fence wasn't a fence anymore. The fence had turned into Matt, who stood with his mouth open wide. He had long, sharp teeth, just like the Vashlock. The little sheep jumped right into Matt's mouth, and the sharp teeth came crashing down . . .

Matt woke up in a cold sweat. He must have fallen asleep. It was just a dream. Just a dream . . .

As he lay back down on his pillow, he wondered if his mom knew how to cook lamb chops.

The next morning, Jason tried to talk to Matt again about his deal with the Vashlock. But Matt brushed him off. At lunchtime, he sat with some of the guys from the Ravens, leaving Jason by himself. Matt felt a little guilty—but not too guilty. It wasn't his fault, Matt told himself. Jason was trying to spoil things for him.

Jason must have gotten the hint, because he didn't try to talk to Matt anymore. Then it came time for the Ravens to play another game. This one was against the Patriots from Smithville, the town next to Bleaktown. Before the game, Coach Johnson announced the batting order. He had Matt batting fourth—the coveted cleanup position that every player wanted.

"I think you've got what it takes to be a real pro, Matt," Coach Johnson told him. "Don't prove me wrong."

Matt looked down at his bat and grinned. "Don't worry, Coach," he said. "I can't lose."

Matt played an amazing game. When a ball whizzed over his head out in right field, he jumped up at least four feet to catch it. Every time he went up to bat, he made a hit. On his final turn at bat, he hit a home run, driving two runners home. The Ravens beat the Patriots 13-4.

The other Ravens swamped Matt after the game, slapping him on the back. Coach Johnson was practically beaming.

"You're going to make us famous, Carter," he said. "With you on our team, we'll win the national championships!"

Matt walked home feeling confident and happy again. About a block away from his house, he started to sniff the air. The smell of roasting meat filled his nostrils. He wiped off a string of drool from his chin and ran home.

"How was the game?" his mom asked him as he ran into the kitchen.

Matt didn't answer. He had his face pressed up against the stove. All he could think about was sinking his teeth into whatever was cooking in there.

"I made a roast beef tonight," his mom said.

"Don't worry—there's plenty. After all, you're a growing boy!"

Matt stood back up, feeling suddenly uneasy. He had never really liked meat that much before. But something was drawing him to the roast beef.

His dream about the sheep suddenly came back to him, but Matt brushed it aside. His mom must be right. He was a growing boy, after all.

Before he could worry any more, the doorbell rang. Matt answered the door and found Jason standing there.

"I know you've been avoiding me, but we need to talk," Jason said. He held a stack of books in his arms.

"What about?" Matt asked suspiciously. "'Cause if you're going to try to talk me out of using the bat—"

Jason leaned forward. "Matt, you're in trouble. Big trouble. Just let me in and I'll explain, okay?"

Matt sighed. "Come on up to my room."

Upstairs, Jason spread the books out on Matt's floor. They were all thick, hardcover books with strange-looking creatures on the covers. They had titles like, *The Encyclopedia of Weird Beings* and *Everything You Ever Wanted to Know About Monsters But Were Afraid to Ask*.

"I've been doing some research on the monster," Jason said. "It wasn't easy, but I finally tracked down a picture." He opened up a book and showed Jason the illustration. It looked like their monster, all right.

"According to the book, anytime you make a deal with a monster, you're cursed," Jason said. "So even though the bat might be making you a good player, bad things will happen, too. Side effects."

"Like what?" Matt asked.

Jason turned the page of the book. This time, there was a picture of a hairy beast. A beast with brown fur all over its body and long, black claws.

"Like that," Jason said. "If you play that third game, Matt, you'll turn into a beast."

A beast, Matt thought. *A hairy beast that liked to eat meat, probably. Nice, juicy meat.*

Matt didn't want to believe it. "It's just a dumb book. They probably just made it up."

"I know how to stop it," Jason said, ignoring him. "If we find out the monster's name, you can break the deal."

Deep down, Matt knew Jason was probably right. But he didn't want him to be.

If Matt broke the deal, he wouldn't be the star player on the Ravens anymore. He'd be the old Matt who couldn't hit a baseball if his life depended on it.

But, the book could be wrong, Matt thought to himself. But what if it was right?

If Matt decides to go ahead and play in the third game, go to page 33.

If Matt and Jason go back to the monster's cave to find out its name, go to page 53.

Luckily, Stan had an old van hidden in another cave in the hills that he used for driving around at night when no one could see his furry body. Stan grabbed his disguise from his cave. They piled into the van and headed to the stadium.

They found Mr. Hamilton pacing back and forth outside the locker room. He looked relieved when Angel, Matt, and Jason came running up.

"I thought you backed out for a second there, Angel," he said. "The game starts in fifteen minutes and the stands are packed. You'd better get suited up."

Matt and Jason made their way to the stands. They had asked for seats high in the bleachers so Stan wouldn't be so noticeable. They found him waiting for them. He had the cowboy hat lowered over his hairy face.

"I sure hope this works," Stan said. "I've been getting strange looks all night."

"I hope so, too," Matt said. He hadn't grown any more fur, but it hadn't gone away from his arms and legs yet either. He'd be glad to get rid of it. And it would be nice to see Stan transformed back to his old self, too.

Soon, it was time for the teams to come out.

The crowd gave a big cheer when Angel's name was announced. Matt, Jason, and Stan screamed and whistled.

When the game started, Angel came up to bat in the second inning. Matt watched, holding his breath. But Angel hit a grounder to left field and ran to first. He was safe, which made the crowd happy. Jason turned to Matt and frowned.

"Better luck next time," he said.

In the fourth inning, Angel got another turn at bat. The pitcher from the opposing team, the Regulators, threw one foul ball after another. Angel didn't get a chance to make contact with the ball.

"This doesn't look so good," Jason muttered.

Angel started off the seventh inning with a high fly ball to center field. Matt sat on the edge of his seat as the ball flew up, up . . . and landed in the fielder's glove.

"Out!" shouted the umpire.

"He'd better get another chance up at bat," Jason said nervously. "Or this is all for nothing."

Matt was starting to feel hopeless. Stan was, too. He ate six hot dogs and three buckets of popcorn between the seventh and ninth innings. Then, finally, Angel came up to bat again.

"Come on, Angel," Matt whispered. "You can do it!"

Angel looked up in the stands, almost as if he had heard Matt. He held the bat up above his head. Then he winked.

Angel got into batting position. The pitcher threw a hard fastball. Angel swung . . .

Crack! The sound roared through the stadium. Matt watched in amazement as the bat broke in half.

The ball went soaring over the field and clear over the fence. The game announcer's voice rang through the stands. "Angel Flores has done it! An out-of-the-park home run! What a comeback!"

Matt jumped out of his seat. "All right, Angel!" he yelled. He turned to Jason and Stan. "He did it!"

Matt stopped cold. Before his eyes, Stan was transforming. His fur melted away and disappeared. His sharp claws turned into two human hands. Seconds later, a smiling, smooth face beamed at them from under the cowboy hat.

"What do you know!" Stan exclaimed. "It worked!"

Matt lifted up his sleeve. His own fur had vanished, too!

Matt slowly sank into his seat, transfixed, as Angel Flores ran around the bases.

This had been the strangest experience of his life. And none of it would have happened if he hadn't gone into Sebastian Cream's Junk Shop.

Matt knew then and there that he had to go back. He had to find out why this had happened.

Go to page 143.

"Forget it," Matt said. "It's my bat. I don't have to listen to you guys."

Matt turned around and burst through the back door. He felt Jason's hand on his shoulder.

"Wait up, Matt," he said. "I know those guys sound crazy. But don't you think maybe they're on to something? After all, you know that's not an ordinary bat."

"Maybe not," he said. "But it doesn't make sense. I bought the bat in that junk shop, fair and square. How did a bat get from a secret government lab to a junk shop? It doesn't make sense."

"I guess you're right," Jason agreed. "Let's go. Maybe I can get Mom to make us some pancakes."

The boys retrieved their bikes from the front of the candy shop and headed to Jason's house. The sun was just coming up, and the streets of Bleaktown were practically deserted.

Then the sound of screeching interrupted the quiet morning. A black car pulled to a stop in the street in front of them, blocking their way. Matt turned around. Another car had done the same, blocking the other end of the street.

The doors of the cars opened, and men in blue uniforms poured out. One of the men approached Matt.

"The bat," he said simply. "Hand it over."

Matt didn't hesitate. He took the bat from his pack and handed it to the man. The man turned and got back into the car without a word. The other men followed, and the two cars sped off as quickly as they had arrived.

Matt just caught the license plate of one of the cars as it turned the corner. It was just three letters.

S.R.A.

"So," Matt said slowly. "I guess your cousin Arnold was right."

"Yeah," Jason said. "I guess we should have believed him!"

THE END

Continued from page 117

"You've got to do it, Matt," Jason said. "It's Stan's only chance."

Matt turned to Angel. "You've been watching me hit all week," he said. "Do you really think I can hit a home run?"

Angel thought for a minute. "You're not bad, Kid. And look at how things are. Stan is a beast. We just got kidnapped by a real monster. If those things are possible, I don't see why you can't hit a home run."

Angel winced in pain, and Stan stepped on the gas. They reached Bleaktown Hospital in minutes. Matt and Jason helped Angel into the emergency room.

"You can do it, Matt," Angel told him. "You've just got to be confident."

Matt hoped Angel was right. He and Jason climbed back into the van.

"Step on it, Stan," Jason said. "The game's going to start soon."

When they got to the stadium, they found Mr. Hamilton in a frantic state. He wasn't happy at all when he found out about Angel's injury.

"What am I going to tell the crowd?" he asked.

"The crowd is expecting a surprise," Jason

said. "Well, I've got one for you. Let Matt play. You can tell everyone he's Angel Flores's latest discovery."

"No way," Mr. Hamilton said. "No kid has ever played on a minor-league team before."

"Exactly," Jason said. "Think of all of the publicity you'll get from this."

Mr. Hamilton raised an eyebrow.

"Look at it this way," Jason said. "Angel can't play, so the crowd's already going to be disappointed. You might as well give them *something*, right?"

Mr. Hamilton finally gave in. "Matt can pinch hit," he said. "But only if I need him to. Okay?"

Secretly, Matt felt relieved to hear this. Maybe he wouldn't have to play.

Jason nodded. "Thanks, Dad. We won't let you down."

Soon, the game started. Jason found Matt a spare Hornets uniform that wasn't too big. Then Matt sat down on a locker-room bench to wait. Stan snuck in after the players left and sat down next to Matt.

"You look great, Kid," Stan said. "And I know you're going to play great, too." His blue eyes looked kind behind his furry face and his big cowboy hat.

Matt suddenly felt guilty. He had been hoping

that Mr. Hamilton wouldn't call on him. He was so nervous. But then Stan would have to be a beast for the rest of his life.

He had to help Stan. At least, he had to try.

So when Mr. Hamilton came into the locker room and called his name, he was ready. Matt stepped out into the stadium. The scoreboard showed the Hornets leading by five runs in the bottom of the eighth inning. There was no one on base and two outs. Matt guessed Mr. Hamilton figured he couldn't do too much damage to the team at this point.

Mr. Hamilton's voice suddenly boomed over the loudspeaker. "And now, ladies and gentlemen, introducing Angel Flores's new protégé, Matt Carter!" The crowd cheered and whistled as Matt walked out on the field. He heard a few laughs, too.

They must think I'm some kind of a joke, Matt thought. *Maybe I am. I just hope I don't let Stan down.*

Matt stood in front of the base and got into his batting stance. The pitcher looked at Matt and shook his head. Then he wound up and sent a ball flying to the plate.

Whoosh! Nervous, Matt had swung too early. He heard more laughs from the crowd.

"Don't worry, Matt," Jason yelled from the

dugout. "You can do it!"

Matt's palms began to sweat, and he felt his grip on the bat slide. He took a deep breath and faced the pitcher, who was grinning now. He lobbed another ball over the base.

Whoosh! Matt was too early again.

"Strike two!" the umpire yelled.

Now sweat was pouring down Matt's back. He wasn't going to hit a home run. He couldn't even hit the ball!

Then he saw something in the stands. It was Angel. He had a cast on one arm, and was waving to Matt with the other.

"Be confident, Matt!" Angel yelled.

Matt nodded. He faced the pitcher and gripped the bat tightly. The pitcher sent another ball across the plate . . .

Crack! Matt slammed the ball over the pitcher's head . . . over the outfield . . . and clear over the park fence!

"It's a home run!" cried the umpire.

The crowd cheered as Matt ran the bases. He had never felt better in his life. He waved to Angel in the stands.

But what about Stan? As soon as Matt reached home plate, he ran into the locker room. Inside, he found Jason standing next to a man wearing a trench coat and a cowboy hat. Matt recognized his blue eyes right away.

"You did it, Kid," Stan said. "I'm my old self again!"

Angel ran into the locker room. He slapped his old friend on the back.

"It's good to see you again, Stan," Angel said. "You should have seen Matt out there. He's going to be a real pro someday, I can tell you that."

Matt smiled and looked at the bat. What if he had never walked past the junk shop that day? Stan would still be a beast. And he would never have gotten those batting tips from Angel.

"It's a good thing I bought this bat!" he said.

THE END

Continued from pages 122, 135

The next chance he got, Matt went back to Sebastian Cream's Junk Shop.

He still couldn't believe what had happened with the baseball bat. It almost didn't seem real. And somehow he knew, deep down, that it wasn't just the bat that had made those things happen.

It was the shop. There was something strange about that place.

As Matt got closer to the shop, he thought about what he might do. He could confront the strange guy who owned the place, Sebastian Cream, and ask him what he knew about the bat. Or maybe he could try buying something else, just to see what happened.

Matt paused before he walked in the door. Mr. Cream looked up from the register and nodded at him. His green eyes seemed to stare right through him.

But Matt wasn't alone in the store. Two kids were standing in front of a glass case. They were a boy and a girl, and they looked a lot alike—twins, maybe. They were leaning over and looking at something.

Matt casually looked down. The twins were staring at a silver skull the size of a small apple.

The skull was engraved with deep, hollow eyes and a wicked grin.

Matt felt a chill all over his body. Without thinking, he quickly left the store. Then he took a deep breath.

That skull was definitely creepy. He hoped those kids wouldn't buy it. He had a bad feeling about it.

And he knew one thing for sure. He was never going into Sebastian Cream's Junk Shop again!

THE END